FACING THE NIGHT

Also by Ned Rorem

Facing the Night

A Diary (1999–2005)
and Musical Writings

Ned Rorem

Shoemaker Hoard

Library of Congress Cataloging-in-Publication Data
Rorem, Ned, 1923–
Facing the night : a diary (1999/2005) and musical
writings / by Ned Rorem.
p. cm.
Includes bibliographical references and index.
ISBN-13: 978-1-59376-088-5
ISBN-10: 1-59376-088-4
1. Rorem, Ned, 1923– —Diaries.
2. Composers—United States—Diaries.
3. Music. I. Title.
ML410.R693.A3 2006
780.92—dc22
[B]
2006021538

Cover design by David Bullen
Printed in the United States of America

Shoemaker & Hoard
An Imprint of Avalon Publishing Group, Inc.

1400 65th Street, Suite 250
Emeryville, CA 94608
Distributed by Publishers Group West

10 9 8 7 6 5 4 3 2 1

Contents

Facing the Night

Prelude: Scattered Notes

Laymen often ask a composer, When do you work? They less often ask this of painters and authors whose work seems more graspable than "abstract" music. Answer: "I'm never not working. Even as I sit here chatting of Kafka or cranberries, sodomy or softball, my mind is simultaneously glued to the piece I'm currently creating; the physical act of inscribing the notes on a staff is merely a necessary afterthought."

A diary, meanwhile, is a genre that everyone knows, since everyone has kept one, if only for a week or two in grade school. Mine lasted three months. In 1936, our parents took Rosemary and me to Europe. That journal is an unpretentious (it doesn't pose as literature) preadolescent travel documentary. I resumed from 1945 to 1947. Then in 1951 I took it up again, and sixteen years later much of it was published as *The Paris Diary*. From then on, knowing that ensuing volumes might also see print, the work did pose as literature. (Though can a mode with neither beginning nor end—a constant middle—be art?) To date there have been five published diaries, through 1999; plus eight more books, mainly essays on other people wherein the pronoun "I" is seldom used.

So I've led parallel careers. Not being a specialist like most professional Americans, I'm a general practitioner, like most professional Europeans. Though let me stress that I'm a composer-who-also-writes, not a writer-who-also-composes.

When James Holmes died, on January 7, 1999, I stopped keeping an organized diary. We had lived together since 1967. Now nothing mattered anymore. Yes, I *have* composed music since 1999 (most recently the opera *Our Town*), but that's my bread and butter. Again yes, I've jotted random prose phrases; it's a habit after all.

Such scattered notes comprise the first of this book's three parts. I'm aware of the many repetitions, often literal. These I justify as obsessions which make up the pith of all diaries, obsessions which shift their sense according to their placement. The obsessions are wistful, even morbid; at 82 I grow self-pitying, alas.

The title, originally *Between the Shadows,* then *Even the Trees,* is now *Facing the Night.* Some peers disapprove.

Part II is made of fifty chronological set pieces. Most have appeared before, as prefaces, reviews, letters to editors, speeches. Here too are many repetitions, which (I pray) change meaning according to location.

Several entries on composers were heard at the semiannual obituary readings at the American Academy of Arts and Letters. The melancholy of these readings is always relieved by a certain elation. For, alone among us, an artist does not die when he dies. His work can last for centuries, and that work contains what is unique to him, and is communicable and healthy, though he may socially have been bad or a bore.

The short entries in Part III are program notes, which explain the origin and construction of nine musical new pieces.

PART I

From a Diary

(1999–2005)

"Will you tell the court in your own words . . ."

Whose words would they be if they weren't my own?

"the truth, the whole truth, and nothing but the truth . . ."

That really means: the facts, all the facts, and nothing but the facts. Truth is a philosophical concept with no common agreement; even Fact changes from one Rashomonian telling to the next. Falsification of fact might be sanctioned for the greater good.

Which is why I called my last diary *Lies* — since so many friends, reading me, say: "I was there too, and it didn't happen that way at all."

And which is why I would call the next diary *Truth*.

My five identities:

> Atheist
> Pacifist
> Alcoholic (recovered)
> Homosexual
> Composer

The first two are acquired convictions. The second two are birthright characteristics. The Composer is the only "problem." In our society, he/she is invisible.

A true artist doesn't necessarily see more deeply than "real people." He sees what is always before us, but tells us what we did not know we knew.

English is the only language without gender for nouns. The French don't think masculine or feminine literally, and could as well refer to blue or red nouns. Most of the words, medical or slang, for the male member are feminine: *la verge, la queue, la bitte*. Most of the words for the female "member" are masculine: *le vagin, le con, le chat*.

Moe's art.
  Beeth   oven.
  "Variations Without a Theme."
  An amusing nightmare.

June 1999

Yes or No
  Like French or German, everything is yes or no. Split second. Do I find him sexy? Should I use this note? Should I scratch my ear now or in two seconds, with the right or left hand?

Famous last words: "How do I look?"
            Paris Diary, 1951, p. 40
            Hollinghurst's *Swimming Pool Library*, 1988, p. 120

"A mind is a terrible thing to waste."
  A mind is not "a terrible thing." The slogan should be: "It's a terrible thing to waste a mind." (Although waste is not really "a thing.")

Am reading Simenon's 1953 *Crime impuni*. But is it the crime that goes unpunished, or the criminal?

Nuclear = Unclear
Zeus = Suez

July 1999

Leave an ape alone with a typewriter, and eventually he'll write out all of Shakespeare, by hit or miss.

That premise has always seemed specious. Why not all of Shakespeare backwards? Or in Sanskrit? Yet surely, even in a hundred trillion years, the ape might type, at most, THE, or maybe EHT. Only Shakespeare can write Shakespeare—though not on a machine.

Vocabulary—No two people will write the same review, yet all can be right. Era and stance dictate "truth."

Eli Wiesel, fifteen or twenty years ago, distanced himself by addressing a group of gay men as "you people." Gay writers, on the other hand, in an effort to be inclusive, are always ungrammatical, using "we" for "they" in a phrase, like: "Homosexuals are . . . , in fact we are . . ."

Beckett should not be "interpreted."

August 1999

You can't get there from here.

I have to get up in time for my nap.

Powder = Red wop
Garden = Ned rag

The Nantucket Murderer

Love is impossible. If it were possible, it wouldn't be love.

September 1999

Henry James — Nowhere in his works or biographies is there mention of music in any form.

 The arts don't interact. They are not the same thing.

December 1999

Humans as the weakest of mammals, and the only suicidal ones. We have maybe ten more years.

All great beauty is flawed. That is, excessive, like Garbo's too-large eyes, or Brando's nose. There is nothing wrong with Lana Turner's face; thus it can't wear well.

 A paragraph on death: My invention — but it's all our invention. And with my *perception* gone, etc. When I go, you all go. We each have a unique perception which vanishes when we vanish.

Mae West songs:
> Now I'm a Lady
> O Mister Deep Blue Sea
> I'm an Occidental Woman
> Frankie & Johnny
> A Guy What Takes His Time
> Easy Rider
> A St. Louis Woman
> My Old Flame
> Samson & Delilah (*Mon coeur s'ouvre
> à ta voix comme s'ouvre les fleurs*)

Everybody likes chocolate, and Ravel, and Monet, and ermine, and Mark Twain, and Socrates. But the enigma of bagels and Dawn Powell, Faulkner and Bruckner, Bob Dylan and Berlioz.

Mendelssohn:

Lieder ohne Worte, Songs Without Words. In French: *Romances sans Paroles,* not *Chansons sans Paroles,* as Eugene Istomin said. Romance without words.

"Maximum Insecurity"

Impact, as a verb

Asked JH [James Holmes] if the new Double Concerto should be for conductorless orchestra. He answered, "That depends on who's not conducting."

Enough is too much. But a little too much is just enough for me.

11 January 2000

Dinner here tête-à-tête with Claire Bloom. We wonder how many gays *are* there in the Academy? In music, 7 out of 45. (Plus 2 others who have "fooled around.")

Thinking continually of suicide.

15 January 2000

In the recent (summer '99) *Musical Quarterly* appears one of those how-many-angels-can-dance-on-the-head-of-a-pin essays, this one by Allen Forte on the presumed Gershwin-Berg connections. The funniest connection is forced between "Summertime" and Marie's "Lullaby" from *Wozzeck.* Of course, one can always find what one's looking for, no matter how far the fetching. But why not state the much more evident theft of "Summertime" from "St. Louis Blues"?

As for Stravinsky's so-called *Petrouchka* chord, which Forte says is used in *An American in Paris,* why not point out that Stravinsky had already stolen that two-clarinet polytonal riff from Ravel's *Prélude à la nuit?*

More snares for the French: The violinist took his bow when he took his bow. Ow! he bellowed when his beau bowed, without his bow.

21 January 2000

Quentin Crisp: I knew him before I knew him, having blurbed *The Naked Civil Servant* prior to his immigration here. Then I saw his one-man show, then read his other writings. Finally, we met, through I think Tom Steele. And though we often did not see eye to eye, we remained staunch acquaintances until the end. No one was remotely like Quentin, with his extreme politeness, his un-bitchy wit, and his basic common sense in the form of aphorism. With his death, the world weighs less.

Sunday, 5 March 2000

Fatigue, depression, insomnia, futility, crankiness, dizziness, all growing worse.

Honors pile up, but the world seems empty. Loud neighbors, dogs, broken walls, mediocrity, and computer expertise reign supreme.

April 2000

Lotus Club refusal to admit me for not wearing a tie.

April 13, 2000
For JH's Memorial
at St. Matthew and St. Timothy's, on West 84th Street

When Jim Holmes died at fifty-nine a year ago, he had lived more than half his life with me. Our relationship was more than mere love; it was based on mutual respect, and our professions inter-twined along with our souls.

Fifteen years younger than I, Jim was nonetheless my best teacher. He was, in his way, the more musically studious and responsible: He never missed a Sunday during his quarter-century in this church; and his weekly program—which always moved along—was inevitably garnished with at least one contemporary work. I would show Jim everything I composed while I was composing it, and this music would surely have been less expert without his comments.

He didn't take himself too seriously as a composer. What he composed was mainly to fill a need for this or that service.

I haven't really been here since Jim went away. Tonight, with so many old friends present, it's odd that he himself must be absent. Or is he? Of all the arts, music has the strongest power of evocation. Maybe, for a few moments, he will return to us through sound.

Nantucket, 17 April 2000

Since Marie-Laure way back when claimed that my French was a combination of *Querelle de Brest* and the *Princesse de Clèves,* and since David Plante last week claimed the latter was one of the great books, maybe it was time to crack it. So I opened my old copy (the fly leaf has my name plus "Paris 1953") and began. Numbing, motionless, name-dropping, humorless. Then, beginning on 68 several pages are marked in my hand as texts for arias. I've no recollection. None. Nor do I recollect the half-dozen bedside books begun in recent months, then dropped. I do recollect Coetzee's painful *Disgrace* and Rupert Thomson's shameful *Book of Revelation.*

"Autumn in New York" vs. "Moonlight in Vermont"

What is Walter Benjamin?
    What is Isaiah Berlin?

Serial music = chaos out of order

May 2000

When Louis Auchincloss phoned to ask if I'd accept the nomination for presidency of the Academy, I thought he was joking. After all, this was a responsible grown-up job, while I picture myself as pre-adolescent. But of course, although all children are not artists, all artists are children insofar as they see the Open without the restraining censorship of adulthood. When they start being grown-ups they stop being artists. By this definition, the Academy is one vast nursery, so I'm as logical a candidate as any.

What would JH have thought? And my parents?

As president of the Academy, I sign all letters to survivors of newly deceased members, adding a personal postscript when warranted. These letters are frequent (the Academy is, as Virgil termed it, an Old Folks Home), yet always a shock: the longer our peers live, the longer we feel they *will* live. Thus when Virginia called about Karl Shapiro, another leaf had fallen from the family tree. Though I met him just once, for five minutes in 1985, I did, thirty-eight years earlier, set a poem of his to music: "Mongolian Idiot," one of my very first songs. Was it, as the saying goes, "any good"?

I called the Library of Congress to send a photocopy, since it's unpublished and half-forgotten. Yes, it is "any good"; indeed, I couldn't do as well now—mainly because I did it then—and will put it in the new cycle. Harold Bloom admonishes readers of poems: "Wherever possible, memorize them." I add: "—or set them to music."

In January of 1947, I would have sent Shapiro the song. He pretended to remember in 1985, but, like many poets, he was not really interested. Nor did I especially care for him—his heterosexual pro-army stance. Yet despite ourselves, a "good" song came of the union.

May Day 2000

Always we find what we unconsciously seek. On another day how would I have reacted to this passage from Leonardo da Vinci, quoted by Denis Donahue (*New York Review of Books,* May 11) in his essay on Yeats?

> Behold now the hope and desire of going back to one's own country or returning to primal chaos, like that of the moth to the light, of the man who with perpetual longing always looks forward with joy to each new spring and each new summer, and to the new months and the new years, deeming that the things he longs for are too slow in coming; and who does not perceive that he is longing for his own destruction. But this longing is in its quintessence the spirit of the elements, which finding itself imprisoned within the life of the human body desires continually to return to its source.
>
> And I would have you to know that this same longing is in its quintessence inherent in nature, and that man is a type of the world.

How well it encapsulates the need for suicide in all our lives. (Or something.)

Saw Dr. Pearl today. Won't take the Zoloft she offered, but she brought me a bit back to life.

7 May 2000

Except for *The Oboe Book* (a series of mostly already-existing vignettes), I've composed nothing since Jim died, fourteen months ago today.

Nantucket, 7 June 00

How old are they now, Tom and Lucille? Seventeen? Eighteen? They were full grown when Jim got them from the orphanage fifteen years ago. Lucille, a thrilling redhead still, sleeps on my bed all night and snores. Tom, handsome but with blinding cataracts, sleeps downstairs but is otherwise always where the action is. They never leave the property and I adore their faithful proximity. But when away I seldom think of them. I think continually of suicide. Will they outlive me?

Carole Farley has been on-island since Saturday. Each evening in the Old North Church we've been recording a program of three dozen songs for Naxos, with a Bostonian engineer called Kyle.

Fatigue, due partly to unending insomnia, paralyzes until late afternoon. Cold, cold weather. Nothing seems interesting.

Wolf = Flow
Pots = Stop

When people say, "I've stopped living," do they mean that they're numb with grief? in dire health? having menopause? continually drugged or drunk? But these conditions are part of living, they just don't revolve around love affairs or money. What's more, all artists "stop living" in order to comment on living. Art is a suspension of life. You can't write a poem about tears in your eyes with tears in your eyes, the salt water would smudge the ink.

Nevertheless, I've stopped living. For nothing counts anymore: Certainly not that paragraph.

Only connect? Nothing connects, yet everything's the same, including the big indifferent sky.

Picnic at Hanging Rock is a spinoff of *L'Avventura*.

Insomnia is a nightmare. If only.

"Are you S. or M.?" "I'm a sadist in the parlor, a masochist in the bedroom."

Can you write with style on style?

Eliz Hardwick is nothing if not a critic with style, and so is John Leonard. Hardwick's every sentence is chiseled and recherché, so are Leonard's. When Leonard reviews Hardwick, in the essay on Melville in the current *New York Review of Books,* he won't be left behind. Who can the reader think about when he so lusciously introduces a luscious quotation? (It would be catastrophic for me to illustrate this here.)

13 June 2000

Went alone to see *Gladiator* in the little hall off Main Street. *Time*'s movie critic had called it "intelligent." After about an hour I wondered: When does the intelligence start? Then left.

With those feminists of yore who claimed that men have it better than women, one must agree, but for this crucial disclaimer: Women are not subject to the draft. The draft eats up young males, whether they will or not, forcing them to learn how to kill their brothers, in ignorance of whatever they're fighting for. Indeed, if their male superiors—inevitably above draft age—find women so dispensable, why not form our armies from exclusively female combatants?

Harold Bloom's new book *[Shakespeare: The Invention of the Human]*, though short, could probably be edited to a third shorter without losing a beat, so repetitious is it. But it did send me back to *Lear*, the first scene of which is so depressing that I turned again to the television, at which I gaze more and more without guilt, but with wistful stupefaction.

Nantucket, 14 June 2000

Two or three times a week tears well up, on the stairway near the garden where Jim's ashes lie (would he approve? not approve?), or on rehearsing in Old North Church, with Carole Farley, "Stopping by Woods" composed as a gift for Father fifty-four years ago, or on merely visualizing Mother in her wheelchair. The tears will never stop, because Death makes no concessions; and making no concessions he condemns us to the clichés—the banality of Death!—of our imperfections.

Tom & Lucille do not think this way, purring in their corners. Nor do whales or finches or lice. For these are perfect adaptations to the random logic of our universe, unconcerned with terms like universe or logic or randomness. ("None of them was capable of lying,/There was not one which knew that it was dying!") Only we imperfect humans have invented philosophy, religion, music, and diaries, to somehow lend reason to the non-reasonable — to help us kill time while waiting for time to kill us.

Man is the sole non-rational animal. The sole suicidal and murderous mammal.

17 June 2000

5 A.M. Insomnia to the point of hopeless fears. Anger. Spilled the water from the side table for second night in a row. In ten years I've never done that before. Glass all over the floor. Herpes again on left hip. Weather continues cold and dark, which is great for discouraging the loud and rotten tourists.

More and more records are coming out. Yet with all this fame and honor, I've not one commission. A few bites. Nor do I any longer "know how" to compose.

18 June 2000

Arts & Leisure Section
NY Times
229 West 43
re: Bernard Holland's essay in today's issue:
"Of Music, Painting, and Parallel Lines"
Since I agree with all the points made by Bernard Holland, when he compares the separate lives of music and painting, I was startled to find my name used to buttress one of these points: "Hardly anyone earns a living at composing. (Perhaps Philip Glass; Ned Rorem may come close.)" If only!

Yes, symphonies, unlike portraits, can't be bartered for millions, making painters as a breed far richer than composers. Yes again, our era is the first in history wherein musical performance is valued higher than what is performed. (The Three Tenors make in one evening more than what a reputable living composer makes in a lifetime.) And yes, most serious composers today earn more by teaching than by composing; what they do earn as composers is from up-front commissions more than from royalties.

What I shall now avow may deflate Holland's use of my name, but reinforces his general premise: However successful I may seem to the general public—the one percent that gives a damn—I do not support myself by the just rewards of my labor. My annual income from royalties and rentals of published works is around twenty thousand; from performances of those works, less than twenty thousand; and from recordings, less than five hundred dollars. As for commissions, it's been over a year since I've had even a small one, and as of this writing I've no contracts on my desk. Indeed, professionally I'm at loose ends.

Sincerely,

Ned Rorem

[Not sent, on Daron [Hagen]'s advice]

June 18 00

How do you say "How do you say 'how do you say' in German?" in Spanish?

How do you say "the lilac-colored lilacs" in Welsh?

June 19 00

Food doesn't interest me. I get hungry, yes, and then would rather eat than not. But recipes—the planning of menus—is a bore. Most of my meals are taken alone. Year in, year out, the daily menu is: breakfast at 9:30 of cold cereal, wheat germ, skim milk, banana, no coffee; lunch at 1:30: peanut butter and apricot jam on whole wheat toast, with a glass of Ensure; evening meal (I abhor the word "dinner"—we never used it at home, even as we pronounced Cleopatra with the third syllable sounding "ay" as in hay) of baked potato—sweet or Irish—with salad and garlic, and a touch of ice cream with three Bordeaux cookies. At 3 A.M. a cup of hot milk and another cookie. Never meat, though sometimes fish if I'm in restaurants, which I've come to loathe.

When did "hep" become "hip"? (And is "hip" still hip?)

30 June 00

Seeking texts for Lehmann competition.

Frost's "The Road Not Taken." Two roads don't diverge (though they can converge); *one* road diverges and becomes two—in a yellow wood.

July 2000

"I Am Rose," like "Ol' Man River" and "Singin' in the Rain," can be played all on the black keys, like pentatonic Scottish ballads.

Reading Nijinsky's diary, Sontag's biography, Harold Bloom, Martin Amis. Nary a word on music. The arts do not interlap.

To the vet's with Lucille and Tom, both about eighteen. If, as the vet says, Tom is now blind and should have his eyes removed before they begin to hurt, I can only feel that nature will take her course. I feel closer to the cats than ever: They eat well and thrive.

Last winter I sent him this letter, in its entirety: "If I were Michael Cunningham, I would come and see Ned Rorem," adding simply the phone number. He called and he came. My letter, impelled as much by his jacket photo as by his two very good books, was a copy of what Colette sent to Gide eighty years ago. Would I have written the letter if his picture had been less prepossessing? Would he have written his books, as they stand, if he didn't look like he looks? Artists create according to how they look. And they even create their looks.

3 July 00

I often think about how seldom I think about Mark.

Colonoscopy is set for next Wed. in N.Y. I'm scared. (Hems. Stomach.)

Mary and Barbara arrive today.

The 4th of July, 2000

Fireworks chez Seward and Joyce Johnson, a fizzle. Wet weather. But post-prandial charades amusing, and company fairly brainy.

Why did Joyce's standard non-question stump me? "If you had a second life, what would you do that you couldn't do in your first?" That implies we simply don't have time to become a dancer, or to read Proust, or to run for President. In fact, we do what we do, and have time for all. Am I lucky in always having known what I wanted to do, been able to do it, and been appreciated for doing it? A second life? It would be the same as the first. But a seventeenth, or seventieth? I'd like to be, for fifteen minutes, a female slave under Ramses the Second; a panther; a roach; a blade of grass; a rock on the moon. The question is as vain as the one about cloning Mozart. Were Mozart reconstructed cell by cell, he might not speak the old language; might adore rock music and loathe "Mozart"; might inherit his old mischief but without shape. Environment is all. So is epoch. Go see the last act of Wilder's *Our Town*.

Nearly twenty-eight years since I've smoked or drunk. But the new laws re. tobacco are embarrassing. Oh, what do the French think! Anything good is bad. For the puritans we still remain.

8 July 2000

A new friend, the naughty irrepressible David Sachs (were we fourteen? fifteen?), said, "Read the last sentence of the last of Wilde's *Poems in Prose*." That sentence: "And he kissed him."

All About Eve. In the stranded car, while Bette Davis and Celeste Holm are arguing, as Hugh Marlowe walks off to find a gas station, do you know the music playing quietly in the background? It's an instrumental version of Debussy's song *"Beau Soir."*

Illness becomes you.

For CF Peters (1975)

Music, in contrast to pictures or words, does not deal in facts—that is, in associations which, by their nature, concern the past. Yet music is associative. Of what? Music is the sole art that evokes nostalgia for the future.

17 July 2000

The so-called Holocaust remains the single most nightmarish phenomenon of modern history, worse in scope than Bosnia, or the Tutus, or Ireland, or other massacres where the body count has been perhaps vaster, because it—the Holocaust—was so organized, so coldly legal, so unpunishable. This said, I've always resented the term "Six Million," as though an even greater number of non-Jews weren't also dispensed with: communists, gypsies, emigrants, Catholics, and Jehovah's Witnesses, vagrants, and, at the bottom of the list, pink-triangled homosexuals.

In the weeks following V-E Day, newsreels horrified America with the starved corpses from the concentration camps. In the balcony of Loew's Sheridan I recall high-school girls, safe in the arms of their brave boyfriends, shrieking, as though the images were no more than some new horror fiction devised to titillate them. Nine years later, during a musical tour of Germany in February 1954, with Chloe Owen, I had "affairs" with three Munich beaux, Heinz, Ulrich, and Gustaf, all my age—the age of Hitler Youth. (To this hour I remember the size and texture of their blondish pricks and balls, their "acts," their every sentimental sentence so different from my French lovers hitherto.) In all of Germany I came upon not one Jew. Jewish-American musicians in Paris— Julius Katchen, Paul Jacobs, Charles Rosen, etc.—played German music radiantly but avoided the country. With Germans I met I never once discussed the war, since I myself was not in the war and in no position to throw stones.

Now last night comes a fictionalized documentary on the Nuremburg trials. Alec Baldwin, the chief prosecutor, inexplicably hasn't seen the film clips before they're shown in the courtroom. His secretary has such great lines as, "How could human beings behave like that toward each other?" A woman starts to cry uncontrollably. (Why not a man?) The Nazis all claim they were merely following orders, but not one asks, "What would you have done in my position?" Or, indeed, why was the rest of the world so apathetic for a decade? The Russian lawyer is already seen as a villain, though in 1945 we didn't see him thus. Obviously there's no final way to portray the situation. But this way is pretty one-dimensional. Tonight I'll look at the second half.

Noting that old Max von Sydow is in the cast, I'm surprised he's still around. Looking him up in the film dictionary, his birth date is 1929. My God, he's six years younger than I.

The second half is pretty good, at least so far as momentum and photography are concerned. And Brian Cox as Göring has dimension. But his character's mention of Hiroshima, and Negroes, and the treatment of Japanese-Americans during the war, is never developed. Nor can the definition of Evil as lack-of-empathy hold water.

21 July 2000
(To be read in absentia at Yaddo)

Since my first visit in 1960, the vital solitude of Yaddo has taught me more than any school. I love those 600 emerald acres, and those ten thousand hours of free inspiration. That my tunes should now be represented on a program to honor Yaddo, honors me even more; and that the program should be shared with old friends and mentors, Aaron Copland and Leonard Bernstein, is the best honor of all. As for my new friends, Michael Boriskin, Lauren Flanigan, and Michael Barrett, all marvelous musicians, I send them blessings on this day, and will be listening from afar.

Incommunicado at Yaddo

WORN TOOL
By Stephen Sandy, 18 August 00
For Ned R.

How odd to hold this implement
                    of a lapsed time
whose dated use clings still in the
                    blunt blade and the
gleaming grip—Celtic chimera,
                    brave lion head
softened by hands. Soon even you
                    will be forgotten,
my letter opener, bronze or brass!
                    No one will know
why such a dull stub of a blade
                    found such a fanciful
handle, as if the one who gripped it
                    fought with ghosts.

It's a nice sad poem.

How about another turn of the screw:

. . . as I too, author of these lines, will be a forgotten ghost, and you, dear reader, will be lost too, and this very paper will crumble and vanish, so there'll remain nothing to *be* forgotten, with the sterile planet careening meaninglessly through the universe for another trillion years, during which the blunt blade of steel might, surprisingly, remain intact.

(Although "meaning" and "universe" and "intact" are mere human concepts.)

25 October 00
Spoken at "The Proust Evening," Alice Tully Hall

We are all Proustian, in that we all have a past which alters as we advance. We would like to freeze that past into the present; yet the present, being in constant flux, is ephemeral and, like the future, does not, by definition, exist. Is a work of art the sole example of the past recaptured? But that fixed work of art also changes meaning according to the perspective of each vanishing month. Yes, even Proust's novel shifts in focus with every generation. Still, we are all Proustian, in that, more than any other writer, there is something in him for everyone.

Am I chronologically closer to Proust than anyone here? Well, sociologically perhaps, since all through the 1950s I lived in the mansion of my dearest friend, Marie-Laure de Noailles, whose grandmother, Laure de Chevigné, was the chief model for the Duchesse de Guermantes. Marie-Laure's widowed mother later wed Francis de Croisset, who was Reynaldo Hahn's librettist for at least one delicious operetta, *Ciboulette*. And Hahn, who was first Proust's lover, then his closest lifelong friend, was arguably a model for the composer Vinteuil.

Marie-Laure, just eighteen when the reclusive master died, recalled only that he avoided hearing *Pelléas et Mélisande* lest the image of that medieval forest bring on an asthma attack. Indeed, though I am in awe of Proust's vast compass of insight, it is only in his dealings with my particular specialty—music—that I find him wanting.

Reynaldo Hahn, a first-rate second-rater, composed these two songs as a teenager. They are in the bland tradition of salon music, on texts of Victor Hugo and Paul Verlaine. My own song, "Early in the Morning," on a poem of Robert Hillyer about being young, in love, and in Paris, was composed when I was young, in love, and in Paris.

Scott Murphree and I will perform the three songs without pause.

––––––

If the Proustian program, well-endowed and well-attended, seemed fuzzy and overlong, it was nice to rub elbows backstage with Zoe Caldwell (dead ringer for Anne Meacham, Robert Phelps, etc.) and Robert Stone. They both had clear diction, as did William Gass and Roger Shattuck. I liked least Nadine Gordimer, full of herself, with all the answers. To claim that Proust, "although himself homosexual, was penetrating on the heterosexual milieu" (or words to that effect), is simply not intelligent. Gays spend their life in a straight environment, as do blacks in a white environment. But can a white person write with insight about blacks, or a straight person about gays? That challenge is more interesting.

Equally tiresome is Benjamin Ivry's take on Ravel in the new biography. He determines that the composer is gay because of his subject matter (whatever that may be in non-programmatic music), or key changes, or other "post-Freudian" hooey. Ivry, who doesn't write well, has made rather an autobiography out of his biography.

To the Philharmonic with Barbara [Grecki]. Colin Davis conducted Schubert, Mozart, Haydn. What was an Englishman bringing this to us for? What indeed were we doing there?

Thomas Adès as invention of the British, as icon to replace Britten. His utter misreading of Tennessee [Williams]'s "Life Story."

The Contender—a good well-played film for the first ¾ths. Then a cop-out. Her defense of the military. Her admission to the President that she *was* set up, and never blew the frat boys (the photos are faked), while the bulk of the movie would suggest that so what if she did. And the corny upbeat ending, disproving the force of the rest of the film: that no matter what, a woman can't make it in this man's world. At least the outcome should have been a question mark.

"An artist's greatest danger is sincerity: If we'd been sincere for even a second, we'd only have managed to have written Wagner's music."

> *Ravel,*
> *To Frank Martin*

A portrait of M.A.T.

17 Nov. 00

Father's 106th birthday.

Continued depression and fatigue, despite continued performance and commissions. And despite Mark, 38 years younger than me.

It's age. I've said all I have to say. Have I?

Pupils Slip Up

More sound-alikes: "My Heart Belongs to Daddy" and "I Love Paris."

In the paralyzing, nightly insomnia, do I sometimes dream that I'm awake?

26 Nov. 00
For Eugene

I'm not a great pianist, but I *am* a good mimic. When people say, "Why Ned, how well you play," I answer, I can't really play at all, I'm just doing an imitation of Eugene Istomin.

The imitation began fifty-seven years ago when, as a student at Curtis, I roomed just above Gessel's florist shop, and just below the Istomin family. During those months of 1943, I absorbed, through the ceiling, every nuance of Eugene's *Waldstein* and his Brahms's B-flat. (The French repertory would come later.) As a performer, he claimed to have been mainly influenced by Heifetz; Eugene longed to produce on a keyboard the subtle portamento of a violin. Similarly, still today, when I write a song—be it on the poetry of Ashbery or the prose of Freud—the vocal line is always nudged less by the manner of another composer than by my childhood pop singers like, say, Billie Holiday or, who knows, even by Eugene's own mother, Feira, who so beautifully sang Russian folk tunes to her son's able accompaniment.

Two of the songs from back then will be heard now from soprano Laquitta Mitchell. They represent a tale of two cities. "The Lordly Hudson," on verses of Paul Goodman (whom we all knew and loved), is an enthusiasm for our native Manhattan. Eugene used to play it with the amateur crooner, John Myers. "Early in the Morning" is on a poem by Robert Hillyer.

1 Dec. oo

Continuing depression. Going through the motions. Nothing matters (except "Will MT call?"). No interest in work. Vaguely fearful of AIDS. But don't want to die.

2 Dec. oo

Ditto.
    When MT is my age I'll be 117.

13 Dec. oo

WBAI vs. Bush
    Gogol = surrealist

20 Dec. oo

Insomnia—depression
48 hrs. without sleep
        Ambien, Prozac
Conjunctivitis (r. eye)
Cough and cough medicines

Fever (98.6 norm) 99.8
Nosebleeds
Sinus
Sore throat
L. forearm
L. foot
Tongue
Herpes in crotch at 2 A.M.
Last night: 1 P.M. Ambien 5 mg.
    v. dizzy

PSA
HIV blood test
Mark's health certificate
Sex ("unsafe")

                                        27 Feb. 01
A. R. Ammons is dead. Like all the others, he is younger than I.
I've passed the age when one dies young.
    Knock wood. And the house caves in.
    Roaches again. When the light goes on in the kitchen or bath-
room at 3 A.M., they scurry away with such terrified skill that I
haven't the heart to swat them to death.

                                 4 P.M., 6 March 01
Scarcely a morning goes by when the thought of suicide doesn't
loom. The world is only what we make of it; it seems no more, no
less, than people walking through the streets. Last night, having
finished the *Nine Episodes,* Mark came with me through a blizzard
to Xerox the piece on 72nd. I was happy for a while: a composer in
fact, and with a lover. Today, usual exhaustion. The music is facile.
Mark is unreal—the fact of him—but looms large. During sex, life
is suspended. What but clichés can be written here anymore?

Later. Post-partum depression, says Mark. And yes, mostly I do despise my music as soon as it's finished. Mark, not (he says) musical, asks: How do you know what it will sound like? That famous question, so hard to answer. Depends on who's asking.

Sean Connery's enunciation—his "s" is wrong. It's not a "th" lisp (which I'm supposed to have), but a "sh." Since there are an awful lot of S's in most sentences, there's no escape. "Yes, he does like sex" becomes "Yesh, he dush like shecksh."

8 March 01

With Ruth Laredo to Elgar's *Dream of Gerontius*. It lacks drama because it lacks contrast. For an hour and forty minutes, the orchestra never stops playing with the singers: There's nothing unaccompanied. And, except for the "demon" section of 3 or 4 minutes, no fast music.

New York, 19 April 01

After a good concert we go back into the street where a hundred anonymous pedestrians, seemingly aimless, head forward with steps they'll never take again—not in an hour nor a decade. But the song behind us, by Schumann or Debussy, remains here for centuries, like Vermeer or Sophocles. Is that song part of us? Does it belong to us?

The loneliness of the people in the streets. Is the post-fucking depression like post-partum depression because we are again useless? When we've finished our symphony, our purpose evaporates. When M. is inside my body, time stops; when I swallow his semen, there is a flash of meaning. Then sadness. Last Easter Sunday, he took me to the Emergency of Nantucket Cottage Hospital because of post-intercourse violence to the rectum. We were the only customers that afternoon, and the all-female staff was helpful.

Write on the Holocaust: How I feel about it today, and the Germans. Like horses, they are "the other."

21 April 01

People sometimes ask if musical ideas come to me, or do I seek them. Well, probably I seek to make them come. If the idea appears in the night—the sleepless night—I recall it visually, not sonorously; I inscribe the notes (or chord or rhythm) on an imagined staff, then photograph the staff, and develop it the next day. But obviously if I'm at work on a string quartet or a flute concerto, I don't attract themes meant for bass drum or harp. We seek what we need.

With Ruth Laredo last night to a pretty good performance, at MSM [Manhattan School of Music], of *Rape of Lucrece*. Britten knows what he's doing; with so few notes, so much "meaning." But the Christianizing at the very end is fatal. Life has no meaning, there is no God; our tragedy—if that's the word—is in having invented Him to make sense of this vale of tears. Now if the opera had ended five minutes sooner, the bleak horror would have been far stronger.

Continual undercurrent of hemorrhoids.

24 April 01

Mark, in despair at losing 2 clients, takes it out on me.

27 April 01

Is one allowed to admit this?

Since I'm supposed to be composing another string quartet (this one for the Yings in Rochester), it felt *indiqué* to listen again to some late Beethoven, after all these decades. So I got the score and CD of opus 132, which I'd studied so thoroughly way back when. And was bored.

When I tell this to people, they act as though I'd desecrated the holy grail, or worse—that I'm just plain unmusical. Beethoven (and Mozart and Schubert) is so entrenched in the general consciousness as Great that even those who never heard him know he's untouchable.

1 May 01

All thought lies in question. All decision is Either/Or. The universal is founded on split-second yes-or-no: the sexual sizing up of every person on the subway. Yes-or-no is for each note of your symphony.

Many a wondrous painter or poet cares naught for music, while many a canny music lover seems blind to evil—those Nazis who played Mozart to drown out the screams of the martyrs. As for the "concord of sweet sounds," if that is music's sole definition, painting is a mere juxtaposition of pretty colors, and poetry a succession of lovely words. Mark the music.

June 2001

For Our World

You Can Go Home Again: Notes on a Return to Paris

Full of emptiness, or rather, empty of fullness.

    The identical view, or smell, or taste, takes on new meaning every hour.

    A tourist in my home town

————

The present becomes the past, even as these words are being written.

    PARIS. Those five letters evoke for us—the twenties. Americans —until 1952. Rosenbergs. *Raconter ma vie* 1949–1964. Then today. The outside is all the same.

    It's still light at 10:30 P.M. Paris is parallel to Montréal.

    All my friends are dead. Will the language itself be dead, as they all fear?

    The gay Marais. They stand in great clusters, youngish with

shaved heads and unshaven cheeks, beer in hand, on sidewalks outside the bar-cafés.

The new mayor, out-of-the-closet Delanoe.

The universe changes permanently every millisecond, and differently for each sentient being. The Paris of my youth is vanished and forgotten forever.

Socialist. No chic. Shared speech on one tone. No "garçon" or "concierge." *On dit "Monsieur" et "Gardien."*

ML's house. It's inanimate and empty and unchanging. Yet my photo of it is not the same as yours.

No car alarms. But loud police sirens sounding a repeated perfect fourth.

English food is (now) far better than French.

11 Place des États-Unis is not so much haunted as decimated.

Paris. It's no longer filled with ghosts; they were laid during the last visit in 1983. It's filled with emptiness.

Paul Bechert's intense letters after fifty-two years. (He's been in heaven for fifty of those years.)

No to all ornamentation in Bach keyboard works. (Like *no* to percussion.)

No to women's clog heels (120 clunks a minute) and cell phones.

Yaddo, 4 August 01

I've already said everything I have to say. Including that sentence.

Talk of translation from the French at breakfast, after a sleepless constipated night. The secret of good translation lies in knowing your own language more than knowing French. There is always an inevitable equivalent, but what is it? The false friends. *Sinistre* never means sinister, but usually means dreary. (Sinister would be *terrifiant.*) *Terrible* doesn't mean terrible so much as terrific.

(Terrible would be *mauvais*.) *Malicieux* means sly. *Vicieux* means excessive. *Formidable* means terrific, or, in today's parlance, "cool" (or, indeed, "hot").

Trying to get the Flute Concerto under way. But still, after six decades, I don't know "how" to compose a piece. Every time is the first time. In the weird Tower Studio, isolated and mosquito-ish, there is a view of the congested lake fifty yards below. The thick moss, the appearing and disappearing fish, the indifferent spectacular trees, remain there, hour after year, whether we're there or not to observe. Or to lie exhausted on the sofa and masturbate.

Rouault. Those four fat vowels all in a row.

Tanglewood, 17 August 01

I am the author of the work you're about to hear, *Evidence of Things Not Seen.*

Three years ago, after a half-century of writing hundreds of settings of hundreds of texts—both verse and prose—I felt urged to compose a summation, a sort of *Art of the Song.* This would feature voices in solos, duets, trios, and quartets. The piece was duly commissioned by the New York Festival of Song, which premiered it in 1998.

The thirty-six songs, based on texts of twenty-four writers, are divided into three groups—Beginnings, Middles, Endings—and were composed during the decline and eventual death of my dearest friend, Jim Holmes.

Tonight the four solo parts are shared by eighteen singers, using three pianists. Their diction is marvelous; but since the texts are complex, you may wish to follow the words.

The piece lasts ninety minutes, and will be sung without intermission. Since it weaves a continuing story, may we ask that you reserve applause until the very end.

I am honored and gratified to be represented by Tanglewood's thrilling performers.

Thank you.

re: Article by Edward Rothstein

In his instructive essay on lies and truth, Edward Rothstein defines "lie" in many ways; he also illustrates how some lies (what we used to call "white lies") are morally defensible. But he does not define truth, doubtless because truth is a vast philosophical construct about which no two minds can quite agree. Nor does he once use the term "fact," as a clearer replacement of "truth," and more logical counterpart to "lie."

But even facts are a matter of perspective. When my music receives a good review, it never seems good for quite the right reason, which is my truth as I experience it. When my diary is published, I lose friends who feel they're misrepresented, which is why I titled my last installment *Lies*.

What would you do if he doesn't come?

Aye wood weight.

T. S. Eliot = Toilets

29 August 01

"Poetry makes nothing happen," wrote Auden in 1939, contradicting Seamus Heaney's current claim for poetry's power against intolerance, as he quotes Milosz: "What is poetry which does not save nations and people?"

It could be argued that some of our great artists have been evil (Richard Wagner's prose was fodder for the Nazis) or, at best, anticlimactic or simply apolitical (Kipling, Claudel, Yeats). Does art change people, or merely make people more of what they already are?

August 2001

Do you still keep a diary? people ask.

Well, no and yes.

No, in that I've nothing more to say since Jim died, and musically too I'm content that etc. But yes, in that a diary is open-ended and life, as they say, does go on. And musically, just because etc.— doesn't mean I'm all written out. I don't believe in inspiration—we're all inspired, but we're not all able to hone that inspiration into something communicable.

Naipaul, Narayan, and Neruda. I've read and admire them all, but blur them in memory.

For Song Class: To Fauré a student asks: "How fast should this song go, *maître?*" Answer: "If the singer is bad, very fast."

Song, unlike all other musical expression, is open to *flexible interpretation.* Transpositions are made for female singers, which would be unheard of for, say, a bassoon sonata or a Chopin Étude.

20 September 01

Heavy rain. To the East Side Sauna with Larry Mass.

Pat Robertson and Jerry Falwell have declared that the World Trade Center catastrophe was God's punishment for homosexuals, feminists, and pro-choice advocates. They have it from the horse's mouth. But I spoke with God only this morning, and He said that Pat and Jerry were monsters.

Homo sapiens may be the most complex of mammals, but they—we—have not evolved happily. Could it be that we've reached the end? That our last great act is to destroy ourselves?

Bjork. Bob Dylan. Oi!

9-11 is miscalled a *tragedy.*

Save the world for mediocrity.

Paul Theroux, *Fresh Air Fiend,* p. xiv, on being "connected":

"We have confused information (of which there is too much) with ideas (of which there are too few). I found out much more about the world and myself by being unconnected."

The World Trade Center, September 11. The vast silence. Nothing will ever be the same (which, of course, is also true when a moth dies in Siberia. We are all interconnected, "even the trees").

Poetry, great art, seem somehow superfluous.

Virginia Dajani phones to say the maintenance crew at the Academy wants to hang the American flag. We disagree. It's too "military." My sister Rosemary suggests—why not the United Nations flag?

Obsessed with sex.

9 October 01

Shakespeare is everywhere, an hourly fact of the international collective consciousness. Just last night *The Merchant of Venice* (quaintly modernized and cut) was on TV; and yesterday also I set to music his 24th sonnet ("When I have seen by Time's fell hand defaced . . ."). But I don't understand him. The older I grow, the less I comprehend: His grammar, vocabulary, images, are far more remote than the French of his period. But then, I don't understand any poetry. Which is perhaps why I set it to music—to give it meaning. Music, of course, in itself has no inherently provable intellectual sense.

Manhattan School of Music, 26 October 01

Because we have only fifty minutes, I've decided not to analyze a piece for you. The music is always available, but me you'll never have again. So let's talk. But prior to talking, I'll do a spoken solo of five minutes (including the words I'm now uttering, plus a reading), then play an eight-minute piece. In the ensuing thirty-six minutes you can ask questions thought up while the music is playing.

I am seventy-eight years old. I am a pacifist. I am an atheist, although I was raised a Quaker. I am politically liberal, philosophically a pessimist, emotionally introspective rather than generous

—although in the long run creative artists are the most generous of humans, and the happiest. I am gay. I am a recovered alcoholic and tobacco-user (thirty years sober). And I am the author of fifteen books as well as the composer of around forty hours of music, half of it vocal.

Nantucket, Thanksgiving Eve, 01

Continuing low. Not working, nor any urge to work. Nothing remains. Our ideas, our eyebrows, our love affairs shift ceaselessly and vanish. In an hour I'll meet Barbara [Grecki] at the Atheneum to shop for a jacket; in two hours that experience (which won't occur as I envision it) will grow blurred, then vanish, like the face of MAT.

But if a thought *is,* then it exists. What exists *is,* goes on forever in some way. Our young daughters grow old, then disappear. Do they? Do their sighs continue through time and space forever, like Caruso's high C or a dinosaur's fart?

Saturday, 24 Nov. 01

The continual false use of "tragedy" for the Sept. 11 occurrence. Weren't we long ago taught that Aristotle depicted a great individual's decline due to a character failing, a "tragic flaw"?

As for art, especially music, referred to now everywhere as a balm, a solace, in these "tragic" times, is that not an insult to art, especially music? Art's purpose is not to pacify but to depict. Are *Guernica* or the crucifixions of Goya a balm? Is *Le Sacre du printemps?* Are Dostoevsky and Kafka?

And Thanksgiving? At seasonal gatherings, must we be asked what we are thankful for? Thankful not to be Afghani or gay or cancer-ridden? Thankful to be American and healthy and straight? Thankful to whom? Thankful to be more fortunate than some other guy? What an egotistical blessing!

My right ear is cancer-ridden. It's unhealed bloodiness will on Monday (if Barbara and I make it back to the city by rented car tomorrow) be reappraised by dermatologist Dr. Seibt. I am thankful for Dr. Seibt in this tragic moment, and will compose an etude of solace.

Actually, I'm writing a suite called (like how many other composers) *Aftermath,* on which I labor for 10 minutes a day, as distinct from 10 hours in olden days.

Friday at 7's, 30 Nov. 01

Stood up. Lonely. Death of George Harrison. *Write about:* Lenny saying "Ten thousand people yell your name. Then you're alone in a Berlin hotel room." The signing Tues. The collegiate choral Wed. The Peabody's (Menotti) Thursday. Then stood up tonight. Why can't I welcome the free time to work and read?

15 Dec. 01

Last night Maggie Paley gave me *The Rings of Saturn* by W. G. Sebald, whom I'd never heard of. "The profoundly elegiac and distinctive author . . ." was killed, like Camus and Pollock and James Dean, yesterday in a car crash with his daughter in Norfolk, England. Tonight I've been reading him.

Well, so much of it is mere description. Elegant and novel description, to be sure, but description nevertheless—which is the basis of sophomorism. Elsewhere it's sensitive reviewing of people and places (Roger Casement, Sir Thomas Browne, the Holocaust, the English landscape). But who is *he?* And can he not pursue any subject to its end, despite the endless run-on paragraphs and the endless use of "I" and "me."

Hey, wait! I see. It's a one-thing-leads-to-another genre. But unlike Proust, this doesn't cohere. Encyclopedic snippets, humane but not human. Stultifyingly beautiful.

Ever more a vegetarian, I hate to kill even roaches as they flee from the sink, hearts pounding, to their loved ones behind the wall. Yet Mary says I'm cold to *her* loved ones.

26 Dec. 01

Kennedy Center on TV. Of the five honorees, only one, Jack Nicholson, was not a musician. The others (Pavarotti, Cliburn, Julie Andrews, Quincy Jones) were musicians, although, contrary to Walter Cronkite's prefatory burst about the encouragement of creativity, they were *performers* who had nothing to do with the creation of what they performed. Cronkite also referred, incorrectly, as so many even-educated folks do today, to the "tragedy" of September 11th. Unless, of course, we allow that America, due to her heroic hubris, indirectly brought about the catastrophe.

Shall I admit that I was moved by every one of the honorees?

7 January 02

More and more withdrawn, as the end (in a month? in a decade?) approaches. Sad—when Sondra's friend Emmett rejects me because of AA anti-promiscuous principle rather than my ugliness. Regular sex would be nice (it's always on my mind). But love doesn't make one less lonely. Does it?

14 January 02

President Bush. Couldn't his accidental fall, while munching pretzels and watching, all alone, a football game, have really resulted from being drunk?

7 Feb. 02

Tristan, with Barbara's German friend, Henning: Socialists and even the economy don't make for *art* in Europe. Art springs (he feels) from tension and unfairness.

Wagner—that Jew-hating pious middle-brow bore—wrote the most successfully "inspired" music since Bach. I used to say, "I love Wagner if I don't have to listen to him." But listening to two uninterrupted hours of *Tristan* tonight caused me to burst into tears. Deborah Voigt is the definitive soprano for this.

My phobia of women's wood clog heels which, clumping on the

pavement 120 times a minute, continually draw attention to their wearer who, impervious on their cell phones, ignore the outer world and the sunshine and the clouds.

Cell phones. I'm forever trapped in the twentieth century, with no fax, or internet, or e-mail, and no feeling of loss thereof.

23–24 Feb. 02

Dream. A concrete wall with eight small holes. Through each hole an eye peeks. The eyes are notes. A voice explains that these notes are by Handel.

Rereading and reviewing *Our Town* with the notion of making with Sandy McClatchy an opera. Would Wilder have penned that play if Edward Arlington Robinson had not existed? or Walter de la Mare (whose "Epitaphs" were so eloquently musicalized by Chanler)? or Edgar Lee Masters?

26 Feb. 02

Death of Leo Ornstein, age 109.

Backlash. Hash-hish. Back-sheesh.

Payola. Crayola. Say: Nola.

26 Feb. 02

At rare theater visits anymore, it's always to ask "What am I doing here?" Years pass. . . . Yet last week I found myself at two plays. *Cymbeline,* updated and vulgar, was yelled from start to finish. So was Albee's *The Goat.* We left both halfway through.

I'd looked forward to Edward's play (for which Michael Erhardt had spent $120 on tickets), but sat there in disbelief. Any new artwork can, to some extent, be justly judged by initial gut reaction, even if it's a "time art," like music or drama, as opposed to a visual art like painting, to which you can turn your back after two seconds and still have seen it entire. After the first minute of *The Goat* it was clear we were in for it: The donnée of the hero's forgetfulness led to endless repetitions of simple data by a loud and hostile heroine. The audience, primed by television, giggled on cue at the laugh-track tragedy. All four undifferentiated characters say "fuck" once a minute, though that word can have impact just once every hundred pages, like an exclamation point. All four seem equally slow in their impatience, and three of them seem somehow mocking in the unusually plaintive notion of loving a goat. Edward, with his famous "ear for dialogue," is self-indulgent to a fault; the dialogue (and the "fucks") may be true to life, but art is not life, it's a condensation of life.

If this play's the best we have, we don't need any worst. Have I always thought this of Edward? Certainly his early economical pieces packed a wallop, nor were they a "dumbing down." And I'm honored to be the dedicatee of one of them. But have they ever been *about* anything—except, of course, Life's Anxieties? (What if it were a male goat?)

How many friends have killed themselves? Tom Prentiss, Claude Lebon, Norris Embry, Bill Flanagan? Well, they didn't do it for me. Cocteau was so often "accused" of his friends' suicides. Yet wasn't it just that, like me, he was attracted to suicidal types?

re. dumbing down. Dave Letterman replacing Ted Koppel. The Arts & Leisure stressing more pop (so Rockwell resigns). My own Boosey & Hawkes being auctioned. Tina Brown. WNYC now a talk station.

11 March 02

Six-month anniversary of 11 Sept. disaster.

Jed canceled our date for this afternoon.

Keenlyside canceled the major premiere, in six weeks, of *Another Sleep*. (He's had the score nearly two years.)

Sonny's ashes delivered today from crematorium in Lenox.

15 March 02

Lucille slept her last today. Barbara and I will pick up her ashes tomorrow. Everything ends. She'll no longer purr at night beside my wakeful corpse. Even endings end.

Our obsession with "child abuse" in the church — is it so important? Paul Goodman and sex. Our smug government. The Army is a form of child abuse.

Fight wars with *women*, and with men over forty.

2 April 02

Welz Kauffman on the phone asks if the two opening intervals of *Aftermath* — a rising ninth and a descending eleventh — were inspired by the September 11 attack.

16 April 02

Relapse. Fever 99+, worse than ever. Ambien again. No help.

The pills aren't doing any good at all. They lower my resistance and make me ache. Constant cough. No sleep. Blood in stool. Weeping.

21 April 02

How many weeks has it been of hacking fever, of doctors and broken dates and paroxysms of insomnia?

I'm without sin. I'll throw the first stone.

That first stone is your first sin.

À *Gout de souffle* translates as "out of breath," not as "breathless."

Diaghilev's famous admonition to Cocteau, *"Étonne-moi,"* translates not as "astonish me," nor yet as "astound me," but simply as "surprise me."

With Renaud Machard, a vain struggle to find the French

equivalent of "cut off your nose to spite your face." He's translating *The Paris Diary*, which will come out in France after thirty-five years!

21 *May 02*

(Toward a blurb for a book of the conversations between Robert Craft and Igor Stravinsky):

In an increasingly dumbed-down world, where the cultured past is fading forever, it is a relief to rediscover Stravinsky's unique conversations with Robert Craft.

Nothing a great man says is inconsequential; all that Stravinsky says is, in fact, consequential. He tells us, in words, what music is, and he does this by reviving (in words) every piece he ever composed. In this Stravinsky is a marvelous historian, reanimating Diaghilev and Nijinsky, Thomas Mann and Ansermet, Varèse and Auden, and . . .

But his own words cannot, of course, delineate why the music is "great." He himself adds: ". . . what can one say about music that is so unmysterious, and so easy to follow at every level and in all relationships?"

This new—or rather, old—collection is a masterpiece of nostalgia, instruction, originality, and intellectuality of the highest order.

5 *June 02*

An ever-higher pile of unfinished books at the bedside. Those authors who so beguiled in previous years seem now just prolix and dull with their "fine writing." Naipaul, Ian McEwan. Rilke's *Letters to a Young Poet* remains sophomoric, stressing "art" and "soul" rather than hard work.

All of a sudden the scenery looks flat and fast, as though I'd accidentally turned two pages instead of one. Without exception we are all insane; our unified ability to curb it is called Civilization. Those who cannot curb it are put into asylums or turned into heads of state.

Depression and insomnia are daily companions. But I'm too busy for suicide.

16 June 02

Drove to Nantucket with Mary. The radio blasted the *Jupiter* Symphony, which seemed endless and unvarying. But it's always a pleasure to stop at the "Twin Peaks" truck stop (route 93) for home-made lemon meringue pie.

Saw and very much admired Albee's early *All Over*. Death from seven tight vantages. What a pleasure to phone Edward to tell him this. Of course he was far more interested in why I didn't like *The Goat* than why I did like *All Over*.

22 June 02

To the Editors
Inquirer and Mirror
If asked to list my ten favorite spaces in America, one would certainly be the lecture hall of Nantucket's Atheneum Library. This unique vast room, with its high windows and raised stage where Emerson, as guest of Maria Mitchell, often spoke 150 years ago, is a delight for both historians and art lovers. When I moved to Nantucket in 1973, the Atheneum was a pleasure to browse in, for its physical appeal and for its cultural stimulation.

How distressing today to find this second-storey area entirely given over to e-mail users and to busy employees doling out computers (to be used for no more than a half-hour). Surely there are other venues on the island—the city hall, perhaps; the high school; the Atheneum's very basement—where these functions could be practiced. The nature of a library, like that of a museum, is to preserve the magic of the past, and not to host intruders whose business is unrelated to the magic.

Well, change is inevitable. As John Stanton's *Last Call* so poignantly showed us at the film festival, things on Nantucket ain't what they used to be. But why must the change always be for the worse?

Nantucket, 23 June 02

Finishing orchestration of Flute Concerto, a fragmentary piece off the top of my head. I've said all I have to say, including in this diary, and wouldn't continue except for commissions which are still forthcoming (though not to David Diamond, with whom I spoke yesterday). Still, what piece is not off the top of my head? Or anyone's? It will be as good as it is. Etc. Though, left to my own devices, I'd compose only vocal music, and only with piano. No orchestra. Spare time? Reading engrosses me less and less. Think continually of sex and, when in NY, go more or less weekly to the East Side Sauna. Otherwise think of death.

Aftermath was finished four months ago and will be premiered in five weeks. I sent the score to the sexy Welz Kauffman, who replied: "Did you know that the entire vocal line of the opening song, 'The Drum,' is built on a continually repeated rising ninth followed by a descending eleventh? Was this conscious?" No. Nor was it probably even unconscious, since I don't "think" that way; nor was the term nine-eleven in vogue quite yet. As for the words beneath the first nine-eleven, "I hate that drum's discordant sound," I didn't consider that a drum, being no-pitched by its nature, cannot sound discordantly.

Tragedy sees two sides of one coin. Comedy sees three sides.

24 June 02

Remember the Kid who gave a blowjob to Ludwig Wittgenstein? Wittgenstein, whose picture in the encyclopedia seemed so male, so sad, so smart. The philosopher, absorbed in work at his desk, hadn't bathed in days, and was still at work when the Kid crawled beneath the table to bury his face in the Master's crotch. He unbuttoned the fly and withdrew the large and already semi-erect member which reeked of honest sweat. He sucked the Austrian cock slowly, but with agile tongue, while stroking the pendulous scrotum. After five minutes Wittgenstein ejected a huge store of white liquid, then for five minutes lay panting. Now he gently kicked the Kid as though to say "let me get on with my work" . . . (Ludwig's older brother, the pianist Paul, lost his right arm during World War I. Paul commissioned a number of works for left hand alone, including Ravel's famous Concerto of 1931.)

If ever these pages are published, that paragraph will be soberly copy edited, set into print, read, sold, etc. The non-intellectual experience itself, emerging from what may now be a corpse, is lost forever, yet never lost.

During sex am I a composer? a Pulitzer Prize winner? a depressed genius? or a one-track-minded slave? an object, not a subject? a thing?

Why?: Dawn Powell. Or Akhmatova.

Nantucket, July 02

Chanel: *"La mode c'est la beauté qui devient laide. L'art c'est la laideur qui devient belle."* (Fashion is beauty that turns ugly, art is ugliness that turns to beauty.)

Discussion on suicide. The Johnsons'. M's avowal that at nineteen she tried it.

Spontaneity needs rehearsal.

Where in the three books I'm simultaneously reading (Frank Conroy, Jack Kerouac, Heinrich Böll) did I last night see the phrase "used bookstore" and noted in the margin "used-book store"? The margins of every book I own are littered with blue-penciled suggestions, even Henry James and Shakespeare.

7 July 02

On the face of it, Judy Collins and I would seem to be barking up different trees in the same forest. I am a creator of dense music in large forms, like symphonies, quartets, concertos. Judy is a re-creator of simpler music in small forms, all of it vocal. Music is *not* a universal language: What we like depends on our environment, generation, and nationality.

But Judy and I are friends of thirty years and share many tastes and distastes. And back in my twenties I composed several classical songs which today seem ideal for Judy. We'll perform three of these now, as a brief uninterrupted group.

"A Christmas Carol" is on an anonymous text from the sixteenth century. "Little Elegy" is on a poem of Elinor Wylie. And "Early in the Morning," on words of Robert Hillyer.

21 July 02
For Yaddo

No one could be more worthy of a stay at Yaddo than Susan Sandler. During the years I've known her—as neighbor, friend, and colleague—she has never seemed less than 100% engrossed in her work. That work is mainly theatrical and very experimental: scripts for the stage, the movies, TV.

Crossing Delancey, Susan's best-known piece, depicts with strong charm the clash between old and new, as society (not always for the better) evolves away from itself. To some extent, this evolution is the theme of all art, and Susan Sandler is a major "variationist" of the theme.

As a person, she is affable, intelligent, and socially attractive. I support her wholeheartedly in anything she attempts.

Dread the morbid insomniac night when I dread the morose ordinary day. Try to read Richard Powers's *Gain* (lent with high praise by Frank Conroy) but find it incomprehensible.

Mary's car, parked in front of the house, was badly sideswiped in the early hours. We await the police.

27 July 02

Phoned the dedicated Margo Garrett at midnight to learn how the premiere of *Aftermath* fared at Ravinia this afternoon. She claims it went flawlessly, is a masterpiece, and that it was preceded by a Bolcom opus on six stanzas of Jane Kenyon, which she read to me. "Let Evening Come" ends:

> Let it come, as it will, and don't
> be afraid. God does not leave us
> comfortless, so let evening come.

Who "comfortless"? the Holocaust victims? the Afghanis? Jesus on the cross? Myself when Jim died? Yes, I too set words of Jane Kenyon, "The Sick Wife," six years ago. The touching poem was in the *New Yorker,* so I wrote to ask her permission, not knowing (as her husband, Donald Hall, answered) that she was dead. She was a real poet. But like so many others, viz. Jorie Graham, so centered on the pronoun "I," that what is left for the reader?

Margo says that Hakan Hagegard has taken my cycle back to Sweden.

What is the aim of life?

The aim of life is to seek life's aim. Next question?

Music is as good as its performance. A book is as good as its cover. This is not a parallel, since music has no cover, and since a book is its contents. But there is no single *right* way to play a piece nor to read a book. Nor can a piece be judged until it's over. (Not quite so.) A picture we can know in a split second, then look away forever while recalling. We can't listen away the music.

Hegemony. Eponymous. Words I never recall the meaning of. Is there no shorter way? The best English is derivative of Anglo-Saxon, not Latin. Virgil used to advise his stringers, "Don't say she had faulty intonation. Say she sang off pitch."

1 August 02

Tom disappeared, not to return for 36 hours. His eyes were bleeding (a dark rosebush? burst cataracts?). The vet again suggested removing his eyes. We decided to "euthanize" him. We buried him in the heavy rain behind the garden bench, Kelvin and Mary and Barbara and me, and cried. Was I wrong?

Yaddo, 13 August 02

A lively likeable crowd, with several other composers. And, in the haunted mosquito-plagued tower, I've finished and copied four songs (on Thom Gunn, Stephen Crane). But depression seems always in the suitcase, and this morning there was blood in my stool again. I am the oldest inmate here.

Write on the Saratoga Performing Arts Center, on Lowell Liebermann's residency, and on Dutoit and Chantal's behavior. The loud and extrovert unwinding of performers after they've performed. More than composers, they eat, and laugh, and tell jokes, and are clever, but non-intellectual. Lowell will play the world premiere here next week of my *Pas de Trois* with Chantal Juillet on violin and Richard Woodham's oboe.

Yaddo, 19 August 02

Daisy Miller. Henry James, the perfectionist, uses "pretty" or "prettily" at least once per page in the story's sixty pages. And "Ah," too. And "ejaculation."

Two weeks ago tonight, Joel McHenry at premiere of *Pas de Trois.*

Dined tonight chez Sophie with Claire Brook, David Del Tredici, Tobias Schneebaum, and Allan Gurganus. I mention Joel—his ex-priesthood, his work with the mentally anguished, his attraction to "older men," though I'm the child, he the papa. Are you in love? they ask. Well, he's dazzled because he sees me as a celebrity, I answer. Can't he love me for myself alone? "But," says Allan, "15 years ago, here at Yaddo, you yourself declared: 'There is no "self alone," we all want to be loved for what we are not; beware, don't pose too many questions, just take while the taking is good.'"

Joel, ex-priest, lies atop me, his crucifix rattling upon my naked chest.

If you ever come to Nantucket, make sure you visit the dump. Our town dump is the chief glamour spot of New England.

Trying to read current "great" books. They all fail. Naipaul, Sebald. McEwan et alia.

Arnold Böcklin (1827–1901), of *The Isle of the Dead,* appeals, like Christopher Marlowe, impossibly to me.

Finished "Another Sleep" today. But it's a failure, a dreary rehash of *Evidence of Things Not Seen,* a half-hour lost.

Should write of Yaddo, of the quite enjoyable short month here, naming names, etc. (I am the oldest.) Eventually, I'll reconstruct it, when the bloom is gone.

Le génie n'est autre chose qu'une grande aptitude à la patience. Buffon in his inaugural speech at the French Academy, 1753 (p. 37 of Arthur Mendel's *The Bach Reader*). I remember it— quoted by Francine, who credited it to, I think, Balzac—as simply *Le génie est une longue patience.* In *The Bach Reader,* Bach says: "I have had to work hard; anyone who works just as hard will get just as far."

28 August 02

Describe masturbation at 2 x a week.
   Depression. Constipation. Metamucil.

3 September 02

Back in the humid indifferent city after three months away. Lonely.
But no wish to see anyone.

For the Academy in May:
   The *one* thing I accomplished a year ago was to shorten this
ceremony by 20 minutes. (How?) Brevity is next to godliness.

Elliott Carter, at Claire [Brook]'s *Dîner à huit couverts,* described
an incident about his friend Auden. In 1961, when Henze took
the stage to accept the applause after the premiere of *Elegy for
Young Lovers,* he failed to acknowledge his librettist Auden who
was seated in the hall. Auden was offended.
   But isn't that precisely what Elliott did when in 1978 he took
the stage to accept the applause after the premiere of *Syringa* he
failed to acknowledge his librettist John Ashbery who was seated
in the hall?
   I didn't mention this lest I embarrass the other guests for whom
Elliott can do no wrong.

17 October 02

Nora Sayre. What she didn't know about movies wasn't worth
knowing. I learned that when we first met at Yaddo in — was it
1977?
   Since then, we met tête-à-tête only four or five times; but any
time with Nora was always intense. Our conversation, other than
gossip, was ever about film, and film's relation to music. As with
dance critics, who (shamefully) seldom mention the music used
for new choreography — much less *how* it's used — so movie critics
virtually never mention a film score. (Yet music in film can shape

[or make or break] whole scenes, viz. the scores of Thomson, Copland, Waxman, Auric, Goldstein.)

Nora and I planned to collaborate on such an essay. But, sadly, we kept putting it off.

No one has ever written about music in the movies, how it's used.

Silence can be so much more telling than sound.

In Robin Williams's *One Hour Photo,* the music is one long exclamation point. In *The Haunting:* one long string chord.

Blood of a Poet. Cocteau, without changing a note, reshuffled Auric's score, so that love music was used for the gambling scene, and vice versa.

Eugene Istomin's treatment of *Theraspheres*

Why Bolcom's *A View from the Bridge* fails:

It opens unmemorably. The "personality" must be established in the first two minutes. But given the neutrality of all the music—which is the *tone* of the language—to introduce a corny aria just to please the crowd—is phony & vulgar.

As for the text, when the uncle kisses the nephew (so passionately, so masculinely), why not make this his gay future, instead of his shame? But Arthur Miller's play can't, alas, be updated.

16 November 02

Fidelio at the Met with Russell Platt. A mediocre production of a mediocre opera.

Since I no longer know singers' names, I'll just say they were all German and pretty good. But the direction, in the cowardly philistine tradition of Peter Sellars (if, for the modern public to grasp the "meaning," the story and décor must be made "relevant," then why not change the music too, and add bongo drums to the classical orchestra?), has been updated to what looks like Nazi Germany, with the stage mostly plunged into darkness, even during crucial arias. And Marzelline, who has been led on by the "boy" Leonore, is left in the lurch at the end, with no apology. The music is mostly jolly tonic-dominant root-position tunes onto which are thumbtacked vocal lines. Some of Beethoven's non-vocal concert works are, as we say, dramatic, but *Fidelio* lacks a *sens du théâtre*. Even as diction should come before feeling and intelligence in acting and singing, so visual clarity should pre-empt atmosphere in mise-en-scène. But the audience should not be literally in the dark along with the players. Some of the prisoners' chorus is nice: about 10% of the whole work.

But does the opera deserve better? Except for maybe 10 reflective minutes here and there, the score is ordinary and without theatricality.

With Mikael Eliasen to see *The Goat* again. Even more repellent than the first time. The dumbed-down audience, preconditioned by TV and high prices, which force them to have a good time, is more defensible than Edward's pandering, with each of his four actors undifferentiatedly bellowing the requisite number of fucks etc. as long and loud and fake as before. (The business about an erection when infant sits on his lap is cribbed from Martin Amis. And the whole idea of the goat is in an old Woody Allen movie.) Should be a male goat.

December 02

Every act, every decision, is a question of yes or no. Am I attracted to this or that person on the street, in this room, at the store? A split-second Yes or No. Shall I use this note, that noun, in the next line of my sonata or sonnet? Yes or No? Whales, humans, felines make decisions. Even a water-bug makes decisions, his tiny heart beating as he races frantically to escape our heel. The Big Bang was a quick decision. All is Yes or No. I've said all this before. (In different words?)

I am well-read and not stupid, but I don't know what "modernist" means. To be sure, in the 1940s when we adolescents reveled in what was called "modern music" (Stravinsky, Ravel, even Debussy), and when concert-goers were geared to avoid contemporary works because they categorically hurt the ears, one may well have asked if the same hadn't pertained to Beethoven. Modern, by definition, means Now (not yesterday, not tomorrow), and can be scary or bland. But modern*ist*—and, good God, post-modernist—turns up everywhere, even by true intellectuals, with never a thought to its definition; it's assumed any reader knows the meaning. Well, I don't.

Nantucket, New Year's Eve 02

Rainy.

Isn't the world ugly enough without having to echo it in art? or words to that effect, asks many a parent. Would they thus banish Tolstoy, El Greco, Alban Berg, in favor of *Little Women,* Grant Wood, Harry Potter?

If I could do it over, would I omit in the diaries all references that might hurt their referents, weakening the very flux of such a book? One can't always know what will hurt; and a warts-and-all portrait is more thorough, more honest, than a . . . I don't mind wounding, say, Hitler. But I never meant to wound, say, Shirley.

3 January 03

Was it Thomas Hardy who had an entire shelf of his own books, sent by strangers wanting his signature, but not returned? I now do likewise. It's flattering in a way, and you can't have it both ways; an imposition, too, especially when there's no return-stamped envelope.

When I used to wonder why certain intellectuals said "this" instead of "that"—as in "This is very interesting"—Norris Embry replied, "Well, this is this."

Talk of Joel.

Continued fatigue and loneliness which no sleep or company can assuage.

Anecdote re. Evelyn Glennie (percussion and morality).

Schwantner's Percussion Concerto would be beautiful if you leave out the percussion.

19 January 03

Though I never buy CDs (the house has hundreds), I bought today for Joel, Bach's *Inventions* and the *Well-Tempered* by Gould and Gulda, both mannered and overpersonalized. Bach should never be played with ornaments, certainly not on the piano. Mordants are used to replace (elongate) the pedal.

5 February 03

Do portrait called "Blow Job Sonata" à la Vidal's "Three Strat-agems." Begin with graffito at Everhard: "I like to blow butch guys."

What is a Jew? Podhoretz: A point of view. Michael Tilson Thomas: A descendant of a tribe of Israel. Arthur Miller: A religion. Marilyn Monroe could always change her mind if the Gestapo appeared. So could a homosexual. But not a black person.

Dead this past week: Byron Belt, Lou Harrison, Douglas Allan-brook, Peter Shaw (Angela Lansbury), Leslie Fiedler.

War, useless war, nothing but talk of war.

St. Mark's Church, 8 Feb. 2003

When Charles-Henri Ford vanished four months ago at the age of ninety-four, it seemed clear that there is no right time to die. Then whiff! another leaf falls from the family tree, and suddenly our world weighs less.

I've known both Charles-Henri and Ruth for nearly sixty years, both as friends and as colleagues. I composed the score for one of Ruth's theater portrayals, and collaborated with her brother on a musical puppet show in 1946.

Last night I shuffled through a half-century of correspondence with Charles-Henri, dozens of letters and cards and drawings. How could I have forgotten our myriad projects for operas, his verbal portraits, plans for sung filmscripts, descriptions of Pavlik's fading health, plus Q & A lists for the revival of *Blues* Magazine? Our final professional intercourse was his cover for my final diary called *Lies*—here!—a photograph against a painting.

Today, rather than reminisce about Charles specifically, let me read you . . .

Symphony Space, 28 March 03

It wasn't until yesterday that I met the Ying family, and heard for the first time my Fifth Quartet.

They explained, "No boundaries."

I'm not very good at extra-musical comment about non-vocal music. Besides I'd already agreed to read from my prose, which I'll now do, saving specific comment for the musical half of the program.

Rome, April 03

"The heaviest of burdens crushes us, we sink beneath it, it pins us to the ground. But in the love poetry of every age, the woman longs to be weighed down by the man's body." (Kundera, p. 5)

Can you name me one, just one, female poet from "every age," let alone a female poet expressing her longing to be "weighed down"? Between Sappho and Elizabeth Barrett, who was there writing "love poetry"?

I, meanwhile, long to be weighed down by the man's body (while perhaps hoping to dominate him in speech or in show of musical gift); but can this longing be compared to a woman's 2000 years ago? Or indeed to another man's yesterday? Our longings are unique, like our juxtapositions of taste or talent, or even physical charm, which is always perceived in how we think (have been told) we look. And is refracted by the times, which shift every week.

Do not trust an artist. Trust his work.

Rome, May 03

The nightmare of Rome: Noise, hospital, language.

For years I've been saying I'm morally against percussion: It's always mere decoration, mere color, lipstick, intrusive. Now here I'm about to embark on a mallet concerto.

Thank God I'm an atheist!

Does the Pope wear red shoes? How answer such a question?

21 May 03
At the Academy, on receiving the Gold Medal

I am dazzled. It's the sort of thing that happens to others, but not to oneself. Now that it's happened to me, it's like awakening from a bad dream of our ever-more-philistine world into an ever-smaller community of friends who care about what I care about. Thank you.

Nantucket, July 03

Lou Reed on the Charlie Rose show. He makes Bob Dylan sound like Maria Callas. Sophomoric lyrics, simplistic tune and chords. No voice, no nuance, no charm, no music. What do they find in him? in Dylan?

Nantucket, July 12, 03

Alone in the heat. AA last night on Cherry Street. Formulaic. Hopeless insomnia. 2:30 A.M. one Ambien (5 mg.). Ambien works for about an hour and a half.

13 July 03

Sins of translation. In the current *New Yorker*, Julian Barnes reviews Houellebecq's novel as rendered into English by one Frank Wynne. Barnes quotes:

> As I stood before the old man's coffin, unpleasant thoughts came to me. He had made the most of life, the old bastard; he was a clever cunt. "You had kids, you fucker," I said spiritedly, "you shoved your fat cock into my mother's cunt."

Well, this is not English. In French the noun *con* does mean "cunt," but the adjective *con* means "fool" or "jerk" or, as we say, "asshole." *Il est con* can only be translated as "he's a jerk," not "he's a cunt" which means nothing in English.

Elsewhere Barnes quotes in translation, regarding France: "a sinister country, utterly sinister and bureaucratic." But *sinistre* in French is best rendered as "dreary." The fact that Wynne does not know this, nor Barnes, makes them both undependable. The worst translations are those wherein we can tell what the original must have been. For instance, in *Madame Bovary* Steegmuller translates as "the key of G" what would have been "la clef de sol," which, in fact, means the Treble clef. Etc.

July 25, 03

For Indiana, as a "Living Legend"

Growing older, short-term memory dims, while long-term memory sharpens. In another year I'll be able to reconstruct my whole life up to the age of six months. It was then that I left Indiana for good—taking my parents with me. But surely those first six months are the most crucial of our life, imprinting us forever. Thus I owe everything to Indiana, for without that state, I wouldn't have come to my present state.

The only other guest here in Indiana that I've met before is Twyla Tharp. It was a brief meeting at the American Academy.

I said I'd always longed to be a dancer: Could she choreograph something just for me, at my present age, although I have no talent? She answered: "Well, hmmm . . ." she said. I said: "I can stand on my head." And so I'll do so for you, if you wish, later this evening.

That could be the climax of the ballet about all of our child-hoods. If Twyla will choreograph it, I'll compose the music, Robert Indiana can design the set, and the narrative can be designed by Messieurs Raspberry, White, Williamson, Walther, and Nolan, each of whom I'm honored to be with today.

Yaddo, 21 August 2003

Went last night to hear for the first time the famous Martha Argerich play Ravel's G-Major Concerto. I've known the work intimately since learning and performing it at Northwestern in 1940. (I was seventeen, the concerto itself was then only eight years old.) Whatever else it may be, Ravel's music is economical, crisp, needing no embellishment or "interpretation" (just play what's written, please, and the piece will speak for itself); *Bref, elle est française*. Argerich played the middle movement as though it was a nine-teenth-century German improvisation, filled with "deep meaning," the left hand always a bit ahead of the right. The two outer movements were so fast as to be incomprehensible. Between the movements, Argerich fussed with her overlong hair, the way Cher does. The performance was glitteringly accurate, yes, but she played all the right notes wrong. During the standing ovation, we — Joel and I — left in embarrassed disgust. Embarrassed because this is what the brainwashed public pays a fortune to adore. Disgust, because her probable fee for one performance could be used to commission a composer to spend a year writing a new concerto. I shall forever speak ill of Martha Argerich — to no avail, of course.

Yaddo, August 2003

I am not interested in food. ("How can you say that, after all those years in France?!") I prefer good to bad, that's all. I like potatoes and tomatoes and peanut butter, dislike mushrooms and Brussels sprouts and bagels, and can no longer eat meat of any kind. But all I truly enjoy is dessert: *crème brûlée,* key lime pie, and of course anything chocolate with whipped cream. No liqueur in any sauce, please. ("But the alcohol is boiled off." Tell that to AA.)

The mere word *food* is self-indulgent, nor did we ever use *dinner* (rather than misusing supper) in our Chicago family. I'm not a consumer, not an acquirer. I am not interested in clothes, in "shopping."

26 August 03

Sixty years ago, on the first floor at 2302 Delancey, in the back room overlooking Fitler Square, Shirley and Eugene and I composed the following poem, each contributing every third word:

Annie bathed coquettishly, dousing each foul gem.

H	Harold
I	ignored
J	just
K	karma
L	loosing
M	much
N	nonsense
O	on
P	particular
Q	questioning
R	reason
S	so
T	the
U	unleashed
V	vulva
W	wildly

X   x-creted
Y   yellow
Z   zlish.

(A to G, and W to Z are exact. H through V is reconstituted dimly.)

29 August 03
Before leaving Yaddo

Moving picture. A left hand adjusts a nail against some wood. A right hand with a hammer hits the nail on the head. A voice says: "This is not the truth. This is not a hammer hitting a nail on the head, but the *picture* of a hammer hitting a nail on the head. Art gets straight to the point, is not life, but a concentration of life. Art is a lie which speaks the truth."

Nantucket, 10 September 03

Sleepless, all alone, rectum bleeding as usual, aches and tears, in the cold. At this moment, Michael Tilson Thomas is opening the San Francisco orchestra season with my *Sunday Morning*, composed in 1977, based on Wallace Stevens's poem of 1915. The music is for huge orchestra and the audience too must be huge. All the commotion 3,000 miles away, revivifying my metabolism of 25 years ago, while I lie silent here. If I die, the music will continue to live—at least while it's being heard. When it stops, it will be put away, then played again tomorrow and for the next three days. Does a painter, an author, say: "I am dying, but the picture, the book, is hanging on the wall, lying on the shelf?" Do these works exist if not seen and read? Music is the only art that exists in time (*Sunday Morning* takes precisely 20 minutes and 48 seconds), but does it exist when it's not being played? Does a dead painter come alive when his old picture is being looked at? You can look away from a picture or a book, but not listen away from music.

In the urine-filled insomnia I pick up Tillich's *The Courage to Be*.

On 143 he writes, "Sartre calls one of his plays *No Exit*, a classical formula for the situation of despair. But he himself has an exit: He can *say* 'no exit,' thus taking the situation of meaninglessness upon himself." Now, of course Sartre didn't call his play *No Exit*, he called it *Huis clos*. The English title came from translator Paul Bowles, who came upon it on the subway.

For MacDowell

"If it weren't for you I wouldn't be me," says the artist to his benefactor. How many hundred times has that phrase been iterated by composers speaking of the MacDowell Colony!

Diatonic = diet tonic

Nantucket, 17 September 03

Don't tell anyone, but I bought a Stephen King novel, with the hope of being diverted. Bedtime reading is so responsibly classy (Barbusse, Goethe) that I've just grown bored with "great works." But after ten pages of the King book, called *Dolores Claiborne*, it seemed that it would all be in low-class first-person narration; as such, even *Huckleberry Finn* couldn't grab my attention.

Andy was fucking Jake, when Jake died.

As the first line of a novel, does that grab your attention? Originally I wrote "Andy was fucking Kevin, when Kevin died," because the name Kevin seemed vaguely more passive. But Jake is one syllable, and jibes with "fucking." All's in a name; a fuck by any other name would feel less good. And opening gambits are presumably crucial, even when they're wrong. "All happy families are alike, but an unhappy family is unhappy in its own way"—the statement could be reversed to more effect: Continual happiness is dull and ignorant though rare and diversified; unhappiness is monochrome and also the rule. Anyway, should the comma be omitted after the fifth word?

Jacques Leguerney I met, chez Sauguet, probably as early as 1949. He was a minor fact of Parisian musical life. But one song, on Ronsard's melancholy *Ma douce jouvence est passée,* had receded in my mind until yesterday when Edmund White sent the CD of Irma Kolassi. If only—maybe he is—he were still alive, to know that his piece is the moving truth.

Don't forget to get a flu shot.

Endless interviews and performances. Still tired and depressed. But better to be depressed and appreciated than depressed and ignored.

I walked around our grounds last night.

Nothing's new, except the gardener's dead.

As mother said, "We'll have to be getting a new one soon, the tulips haven't grown."

And he's alone.

Those Frostian verses were in U-High's *Blue Mirror* quarterly, in 1937 when I was thirteen. They are the only words of mine that I've set to music. In answer to the oft-posed question, "Do you set your own words to music?"

All's in an adverb.

When he breaks out of jail we must break out the booze or he'll break out in pimples and break our heart. They broke up, so they broke off their engagement. They broke off the branch when they broke up the party, and broke into a rage. There was a break in the conversation when they started to break down the door, to break into the house. When the brake broke he had a nervous breakdown. Would the slow horse break into a trot? When he wouldn't put out, she was put out. She wouldn't put up with it, so she put him out.

15 October 2003

In a week I turn eighty. I'm not going toward it, it's hurtling toward me, like a black baseball weighing a ton and with a personality called Death.

When Ravel was my age, he'd been dead eighteen years.

I am forever "accused" of narcissism. But everyone's a narcissist — I just admit it. We all think about ourselves continually, and artists more than anyone. Or what is art about?

24 November 03

Dined tête-à-tête w/ Gore V. at the Plaza. He drank continually (and showed it) while keeping up a continually "thoughtful" conversation. His cane. His paranoia re. the *NYT*. What does he most look forward to now? To dying, since, after forty-three years, Howard Austen has died, he has no longer anyone to talk to.

When we parted, he went into the bar. (Whiskey helps his insomnia.) Yet he's quick as a whip on daily visits to schools, and reprints of his whole oeuvre.

He wants to die. "What'll you do if you don't die?" I ask.

"I'll learn Chinese."

Nantucket, Thanksgiving 03

In his otherwise canny essay on Updike, Louis Menand in the December 1 *New Yorker* makes the musical layman's usual mistake of confusing the performer with what he's performing. "Virtuosity can seem a distraction — as when you find you are thinking about how great the musician is instead of listening to the music. In stories, though, this is never a problem. The whole idea is to make language perform its own little supernatural." It's as though the pianist or contralto were making it up as they go along, rather than crediting Chopin or Verdi. As for stories, it's we, the reader, who are the performer. Etc.

28 Nov. 03

Now I lay me down to sleep,
I pray the Lord my soul to keep.
If I should die before I wake,
I pray the Lord my soul to take.

Is there a difference between "soul to keep" and "soul to take"?
Did Shelley pen this? Didn't I set it to music 50 years ago? How I
despise prayer—the notion of faith in the nonexistent.

Hegemony. Heuristic. Two "h" words that I'm too old to learn the
meaning of, much less how to use them. Thus those who do use
them are pretentious.

Six days alone here in Nantucket where I came to work on the
piano piece for James Giles. I've spent perhaps 45 minutes on
that piece, and the remaining hours watching TV (commercials
mostly), resting but never sleeping, with one trek to the movies to
see *Mystic River,* which I left, from boredom, after an hour and a
half. Great acting now means overacting—yelling. Bored too by
Bernard-Henri Lévy's *Who Killed Daniel Pearl?*, lent enthusias-
tically by Eugenie. When I say to people that there is no creative
culture anymore in France, they all answer "What about Lévy?"
Well, he's the prime example of what I mean.

6 December 2003

Mother's 103rd birthday.
    Record blizzard. Back from Philly after premiere of Flute Con-
certo (Jeffrey Khaner, with Robert Abbado).
    The first movements, with those flat sour crashes preluding
and interrupting the lovely bland strings, are like scabs on white
marble.

"When to the sessions of sweet silent thought . . ."

The phrase is fabricated to fit into the iambic mode. Thought is by definition silent, and a *sweet* thought hardly obtains to "old woes" or "time's waste" etc. The line should be simply "When to the sessions of thought . . ." But then the pentameter is lost. Shakespeare often pads.

For John Simon:

Non-musician writers on music: Mann *(Dr. Faustus)*, G. B. Shaw, Ezra Pound, Gide, Nietzsche

1 Jan. 04

Where did I write (it's not in *The Pastry Shop*): "Nothing lasts. Not love. Not our children. Not even the sun"?

Rich Americans, until about forty years ago, bought oil paintings. Now they just buy oil.

In ten years: Either civilization will be physically gone, or so dumbed-down that we'll be one big happy family singing rock at McDonald's in Afghanistan.

I don't like anything now. "Great acting" is so overstated. Sean Penn. *The Goat*. Brian Murray. *Mystic River*. Shirley Hazzard. *Angels in America*.

Anglophones. They all speak one language and use the same vocabulary. Susan Sontag may have access to a few hundred more words than, say, Mickey Rooney. But it's the order of words—and only the order—that results in the difference between writers or the order of notes between composers. Juggle the same few hundred verbs and nouns and out comes Francis Bacon and, with another shake of the bag, Samuel Beckett. Schoenberg and Ravel built with the same tools.

14 January 04

Balanchine documentary on PBS. As I've always felt: What has he done that's *him?* that equals Stravinsky's scores? that's more than people kicking without reason? that Jerry Robbins hasn't done better?

The notorious C# at the start of the *Eroica* is to the ear an innocent D-flat which changes its mind before modulating into the key of A-flat.

16 January 04

Two days with six colleagues at the Academy to hear some seventy tapes of hopeful composers. Not one remains in the memory. Nearly all wrote "effects." Flutter tongue, col legno, tremolo, spiccato. No one writes tunes, no one composes just music. Where was it that Susan Sontag said (was it an essay on John Waters movies?), "It depicts every possible sexual position, with the notable exception of straight screwing."

    Astray. Ashtray.
    Pupils. Slipup
    Yoga = A goy
    Ned Rorem = Merde Ron
                 Order Men
                 Drone Mer
                 Rome Rend
                 Rend More
    Boston = Not sob

8 Feb. 04
The Grammys

2 1/2 hours of dumbed-down expensive mediocrity. Although I was up for three awards (for the Serebrier recording), nothing relating to classical music was alluded to. Like the panel for "serious

music" at the Academy a month ago, this is all *effect*. And the word "music" today means "pop music."

3 April 04

As the years ooze by the less I literally understand "great litera-ture." In Shakespeare, the grammar, the word order, are baffling. With "Sailing to Byzantium," long since memorized, I just don't know what Yeats is talking about. I don't understand TV either, but gaze at it for hours on end.

In his current movie guide, Leonard Maltin states, under *Mata Hari,* "Highlight(s): Garbo's exotic dance sequence . . ." But didn't June Knight do the dancing for Garbo?

Answer these most-asked questions to a composer: Do you hear all those notes in your head? Do you write at the piano? How do you write for an instrument that you don't play? How do you orchestrate? If we had learned music basics in grade school, like rhyming cat with rat, or painting little pictures, the questions would not be mysterious.

Someone asks, "Do you still keep a diary?" But I never did, I always do. Every once in a while I'll jot something down that might be polished, or folded into a journal. But since Jim died nothing seems to matter. Did things ever matter?—even astronomy, Da Vinci, Lana Turner, or peanut butter? We use it all to kill time while waiting for time to kill us.

31 May 04

Having for so long derided Schubert (those two syllables cause a big yawn) to smart friends who love him, I decided to "try" him again. But in re-reading the B-flat Sonata—the one which begins with an upbeat which to the ear is a downbeat—life seemed too short for such endless primary chords and tunes repeated literally.

He just can't stop. If *Winterreise* is a flawless masterpiece, that's because the pre-existing texts impose limits of the sonic framework. Incidentally, Wilhelm Müller is not mentioned in my edition of the cycle (International Music Company, 1961 ed.); the poet is as dispensable as, elsewhere, the composer is for, say, a listing of *Oklahoma!* in *TV Guide*.

Yaddo, Friday the 13th of August, 2004
Another crack at *Don Quixote*. Am up to p. 209, including the preface by the pretty-good translator, Samuel Putnam. But why is it great? or indeed "the greatest novel ever written"? There are certain works whose greatness I admit, without needing (Beethoven, Gaudí, Faulkner). But another category is "unfathomable greatness" (Bruckner, Pollock, Dawn Powell, Bob Dylan . . .). Now Cervantes falls into that category. Well, I'll give him another 209 pages, to find if there's more than the endless examples of the knight's delusions and his squire's credulity.

I don't mean anything I say. Including that sentence.

Life is German, death is French.

If we outsource when we party, will this impact the downsizing of post-modern software?

Which witch?

"Record" is pronounced differently as a verb than as a noun.

Picasso: "Every artist is half man and half woman, and the woman is insufferable." Nothing is more "German" than to analyze a *bon mot*. But does Picasso's quip apply to female artists?

"Singing in the Rain" is entirely pentatonic. Thus any non-pianist can learn to play it on the black keys in five minutes.

Is it mere coincidence that Kander's "New York, New York" jibes so closely to Herb Brown's tune, even to the little added riff which accompanies the voice?

Club de femmes is listed nowhere in cinema books. Jacques Deval's film, c. 1936, with Josette Day, Danielle Darrieux, has sunk without a trace. Yet it taught me how to bathe with a sponge after a lesbian encounter. Deval's wife: Else Argal?

Islander = I slander

You'll all die but me, since I invented you, and also invented God and death.

When anyone goes, their unique vision (of the universe, of the color blue, of hate) goes with them.

The best of Sondheim's songs are built around the rising fifth: "Send in the Clowns," "I Remember Sky," "There Is No Other Way" (from *Pacific Overtures*).

Postwar, 3 gay goyim: Truman C., Tennessee W., and Gore V., succeeded the straight Jewish, Roth, Mailer, and Miller.

To be "thankful" on Thanksgiving. Why be thankful for anything? For talent, for health, money, intelligence, for anything? Thankful to whom? God? Or even oneself?

Is one thankful not to be a hunchback, or a sissy, or a pauper?

Nantucket, New Year's Morning, 2005

Insomnia.

But aren't you used to it by now?

Does one get used to crucifixion?

29 January 05

Pelléas at the Met. Horrible "relevant" production, with singers doing arias *à l'italienne*. The orchestra was *good*—James Levine.

5 February 05

Charlie Rose—when he does engage a musician, it's Pollini, (??) who never once mentions composers, or Masur, who speaks (in hushed tones) only of Beethoven and the miracle of a *deaf* composer, as though composers . . . etc.

View from the window at 4 A.M. = homeless looking through garbage.

Huge roach in kitchen.

And the Sherith Israel Synagogue. They want to build a 14-story building next door, and we can legally object only on "esthetic" grounds: Will the new structure coincide with the beauty of our block? To hell with the noise and the darkness. Like being burned at the stake in a field of lilacs.

I command you to rape me.

Nantucket, 5 March 05

Insomnia. Every night of the year. Yet every time's the first time.

I reach toward one of the dozen half-finished books on the night table. Wittgenstein quotes Schiller: *"Ernst ist das Leben, heiter ist die Kunst,"* translated as "Life is serious, art is gay." Marie-Laure had the phrase clipped to her easel: *"La vie est grave, l'art est gai."* For me it should read, "Life is aimless, art is order."

Taking *Bleak House,* Dickens in his preface quotes a Shakespeare sonnet:

> My nature is subdued
> To what it works in, like the dyer's hand:
> Pity me, then, and wish I were renewed.

But what does this mean? More and more I understand Shakespeare less and less, words, words. Didn't Auden title a collection *The Dyer's Hand?* Like "Only Connect." What does it mean?

The all-knowing Auden again, in his intro to Goethe's *Werther*, is wrong when he calls the hero "a horrid little monster."

Not being able to fall back to sleep, I make these notes.

In 1946, Britten visited our class at Tanglewood. We asked him the meaning of "Old Joe has gone fishing and you know has gone fishing," rousingly repeated by the chorus. He said that the librettist (Montague Slater) was unobtainable, so he (Britten) just fitted in any words until the real thing came along—which it never did. Like "Tea for Two."

George Perle can read upside-down.

"Pennies in a Stream"
"Moonlight in Vermont"
"Autumn in New York"

April 2005
Pope Benedict, without becoming left-wing, could be the first Pope since the days of Dante, Michelangelo, of Bach, to commission serious works of Art.

George Bush, without becoming left-wing, could have taken three million out of his multi-million-dollar Inaugural Party to commission three young composers to write new operas for the Met.

3 April 05
There is nothing a composer can say about his music that the music itself can't say better, except how it came to be written.

The present work was commissioned in 1973 by a choir in

Kansas. I chose the text because it spoke to my condition at the
time—and still does. Thomas Nashe, a contemporary of Shakespeare's, wrote *In Time of Pestilence* seven years before his early
death in 1601. The six brief stanzas concern the inevitability of
death for all, great and small. The phrase "brightness falls from the
air," I had seen quoted in Joyce's *Portrait of the Artist as a Young
Man* and was thrilled.

The music, divided like the verse into six madrigals, lasts about
seven minutes.

Sound-alikes:

Ravel's *"Air de l'enfant"* in both tune and harmony for three
measures (at 74) and Puccini's *"Un bel di"* (at 14), in both harmony
and tune for three measures.

What kind of oven is a beeth oven?

Art is a matter of opinion, not of fact. No one can prove that
Mozart is good or that Eminem is bad.

6 April 05

How many others in this crosstown bus are musing on the beautiful setting, by Léo Préger in 1949, of Louise de Vilmorin's *Étude*,
which ends:

> *J'ai rendu le dernier soupir,*
> *Seigneur écoutez la prière*
> *De celui qui voudrait dormir,*
> *Fermez mes rouges paupières*
> *Car j'ai grand sommeil de mourir*

4 May 05
For Dr. Gerson

—Little accidents (cuts, tripping)

—Cell phone (on body)

Xanax & Ambien (allergies, sneezing, dizziness, exhaustion, headache)

Insomnia 4½ hours a night, up to pee 5 times, retention/urinary

Herpes

Blood (& blood on shorts) Citrucel and other lotions

Acid reflux while eating/need to belch

Tinnitus

Headache

Tongue

Itch/Rash

Tums

18 May 05

At the Academy today, in the presence of all the members including fifty composers and another twenty youngsters about to receive awards, Elliott Carter presented to James Levine a medal for Distinguished Service to the Arts. Levine acknowledged his appreciation for receiving the honor "from our greatest living composer." Now, since there are no absolutes in art, another could as justly assert that Carter is not only not "our greatest," he's not even a composer.

Endless depression. Death closing in. Body closing down. The world grows noisier. Insomnia, fatigue, sore tongue, tinnitus, urinary obsession. I never write of Mary Marshall or Barbara Grecki or Don Julien, but they are such a help. Although, as Lily Tomlin says, "Well folks, we're all in this . . . alone."

Half-through with orchestration of *Our Town*.

The dead. Bruce Phemister. Ruth Laredo. George Rochberg. We're on the list.

1 July 04

You are my husband but I'm not your wife.

"No one can go through it twice. This kind of a love affair can really happen only once in a man's life. After that he is calloused. He is no longer capable of so many torments."

Thomas Merton
re. his first romance, age 16
The Seven Story Mountain

"And love is always a game. And an invention. And what we learned in the last affair trains us what to unlearn in the next; yet when the next's over we realize that what we refrained from was just what should have been done."

Ned Rorem
In "Letter to Claude" (1957)

"You write in order to change the world."

James Baldwin

"Poetry makes nothing happen."

W. H. Auden

Young = gnu oy

Nantucket, 20 July 05

Twelve hours. What to include? Three incidents? Eighteen? A trillion? Each fraction of a second in each scientist's or mosquito's life in this expanding universe contains endless reactions, and endless perceptions of those reactions. How many layers, and layers upon layers, can be noted here? To omit one just might be *the* one.

Yesterday the humidity continued with no end in sight, and I, dizzy from no-end-in-sight insomnia. Spoke with Jack Larson and with Mart Crowley in California about the death of Gavin

Lambert. Spoke with James Lord in Paris about a documentary on French Television of Marie-Laure. On local television at two o'clock was a conversation with me, but we missed it. At eight o'clock, went alone to hear The Western Wind, a six-part a-cappella ensemble (in tune, but with fair diction), do an American program, including NR's and Paul Goodman's "Creator Spirit." At eleven o'clock watched Charlie Rose's interview with Larry Kramer and the latter's conviction about our nation's increasing homophobia. Retired at midnight as usual, and as usual read until 12:25 (Thomas Merton's *Seven Story Mountain*). Slept as usual until 1:30, then awake till 2:30 when I took an Ambien (5 mg.), which I do every two or three nights.

Should it be added that Ambien has no desired effect? I still rise every seventy minutes to pee (a mere dribble), staggering to the bathroom where I hear laughter in the toilet.

Should it be added that Larry Kramer bases his proof of homophobia in the 70 billion dollars allotted but never sent to AIDS victims in Africa? But these victims are largely women and children and not necessarily gay. And even if the world could kill all gays, the same percentage would continue being born. (A third layer would be my early meetings with Kramer.)

Could it be added that at the choral concert there was a person (now with his wife) whom I knew 40 years ago through Glenway Wescott? (Other layers: Wescott and Robert Phelps. Phelps and my first diary. Paul Goodman)

And should it be added that James had . . . ? That Gavin reviewed (my first review for prose) the *Paris Diary* in 1967? That . . .

That Thomas Merton's family book goes against my grain. Yes, his chapter on France (p. 33) is good. But there's bad writing too, and a need to hurry him up. His thoughts on Quakers are shallow. And any talk of God as our savior increasingly appalls me; we've invented him out of need. To disagree with someone intelligent seems more hopeless than to disagree with a fool. (On page 137 the word "all" appears twelve times.)

Jim Crace — His books are beautifully short, yet they're too long. Every word is in place, yet there are too many. He makes the same point too many times, and (though he may not realize it) often in iambic pentameter.

Beethoven and Satie? They are brothers, at least here: [Several measures from Beethoven's opus 135 and from a *Gymnopédie*]

Neighbors say their brother sings my songs. The "songs" turn out to be the choral "How lovely is thy dwelling place." Yes, I know it by heart. But when did I pen it? Who prints it? I can find it listed nowhere.

Likewise "We are the music makers."

Signals = slang is

Saw about twenty minutes of *Queen Christina,* which I'd not experienced since 1933, age nine. The recollection was indelible, even to a "false relation" toward the end. Garbo, quite masculine throughout (long strides, folded arms), seems to be waiting atop the palace stairs. A loud revolutionary band of all-male civilians, armed with torches, mount the steps, then stop abruptly at the sight of their queen. Garbo slowly approaches. "What do you do?" she asks the head man. "I am a blacksmith, your majesty, like my father, and his father's father." The queen: "I would not tell you you are a bad blacksmith. Do your work and I will do mine." The false relation is that they're equals, and that their jobs correlate. In fact, the queen's job, by its nature, affects all their lives; the blacksmith's affects only his small milieu.

Similarly, in *Lost Horizon,* the revitalization of Shangri La — Earth's ideal location where mutual love fuels the beauty of longevity—is effected only by kidnapping the passenger of a plane who will bring new blood to Eden, and by murdering the pilots.

"Two roads diverged in a yellow wood, . . ." states an impossibility. *One* road diverges into two. Is that correct?

Suicide note. Tomorrow will be like today. The men will get up and go to work again. Those green needles at the top of the 80-foot pine will be wafted by that high wind as they are wafted now. Those women across the way will go back to the grocery store, and the cats will race after them. The wisteria smell at dusk will be inebriating. The sun will rise once more, as the television sends out more pictures of a hopeless war. Everything will be like today. Only I won't be here to see it.

PART II

Collected Writings

(1993–2006)

Notes on Marc

Inside every composer lurks a singer longing to get out. What is called "the composer's voice"—that squeaky unpitched organ with which composers audition their vocal works to baffled sopranos or uninterested producers—may explain their becoming composers in the first place: the vengeance of frustration. The human voice is, after all, both the primal and the final expression, the instrument all others seek to emulate. We are what we sing; any music worthy of the name is inherently sung, whether it be for tenor or tuba or tambourine.

During my growing-up period I knew only two exceptions to the rule that the composer-as-singer sabotages his own work. One was Samuel Barber, whose still-available recording of his own *Dover Beach*, made sixty years ago, reveals a gently excellent baritone with the Italianate *r*'s still favored by the few Americans who sing in their own tongue. The other was Marc Blitzstein. True, Marc had a "composer's voice," but such a voice that could put over his own songs out of a horny conviction I've never heard anywhere else. Blitzstein, the pseudo-amateur, hypnotized the professionals around him. The whole spellbound cast of *The Threepenny Opera* sounds like him, including Louis Armstrong and Lotte Lenya and Bobby Darin. Indeed, if you want to know the dancer from the dance, you need only hear a "real" voice intoning one of Marc's left-wing ditties to realize that both words and music are lessened by standard beauty.

Both Barber and Blitzstein were raised in well-off pre-World-War-One Philadelphia milieux, veering thence in opposite directions, Sam toward the anxieties of mandarin individuals (Cleopatra, Prokosch, Kierkegaard, Vanessa), Marc toward the collective woes of Everyman. During the Second World War they did both serve in the military, resulting in a jingoistic bomb from each one: Barber's Second Symphony known as the *Night Flight* which he finally withdrew, and Blitzstein's *Airborne Symphony,* which finally withdrew itself. Beyond this coincidence, they had nothing in common. That one was Episcopalian, the other Jewish, surely figured.

A more cogent comparison is between Pasolini and Blitzstein, both upper-crust communists murdered by rough trade, the first in the outskirts of Rome by one of the very *ragazzi di vita* he had spent a lifetime nurturing, the second on the isle of Martinique by the very type of deprived seafaring gay-basher he had spent a lifetime defending. Though communism may have been a mere touristic escape for each man's life, it nonetheless formed the core of each man's art. ". . . A scholar and a master of the Italian language, [Pasolini] picked up no grounding at all in the life of the proletariat," wrote Clive James recently. "He never did a day's manual labor then or later. . . . This is standard for revolutionary intellectuals and can't usefully be called hypocrisy, since if there is such a thing as proletarian consciousness then it is hard to see how any proletarian could escape from it without the help of the revolutionary intellectual—although just how the revolutionary intellectual manages to escape from bourgeois consciousness is a problem that better minds than Pasolini have never been able to solve without sleight of hand."

As for Marc, how might he have reacted to the "liberation" of communists thirty years after his death? By seeing them as eager consumers, no better than they should be? (My father liked to refer to this or that achiever as "born of poor but dishonest parents.") Today we perceive a lopsided focus in certain visions of the golden past. Marc retained the focus to the end, though his friend Lillian Hellman wrote: "A younger generation . . . look upon the 1930s radical and the 1930s red-baiter with equal amusement. I don't much enjoy their amusement, but they have some right to it."

In the mid-fifties, half my life ago, I was young enough still to be dazzled by my legendary seniors, and smug enough to feel a power when introducing, for the first time, one of these seniors to another. The great torch singer Libby Holman had become a friend. She had never met Marc, but would perhaps have enjoyed playing the role of Jenny in *Threepenny Opera* which at the time had made Marc (ironically, because he was only the translator, and because the late Kurt Weill, a homophobe, never cared for Marc's "cashing in") a rich star. One evening I brought them together in a bistro on West Twelfth. Libby, exonerated from maybe having murdered her husband years before, had inherited that husband's fortune, but spent a goodly chunk of it on civil rights groups, especially after her only son died while mountain climbing. There now I sat, silent, as these two conversed intensely with their violent theatricality, their true unusualness. There I sat with her who maybe had killed, with him who would be killed, and her who would later kill herself.

Libby never once mentioned the role of Jenny. Marc paid the bill.

––––––––––

Like most young composers in the 1940s I knew Blitzstein's worth solely from hearsay. Textbooks were full of him as America's embodiment of Brecht's "art for society's sake"; he himself decreed that the creative artist must "transform himself from a parasite to a fighter." A parasite on whom? I wondered. A fighter for what? If I was not political, I *was* impressed by those who were, like Lenny Bernstein and Aaron Copland, who constantly sang Marc's praises, making me feel guilty. Even Virgil Thomson, a sometime foe of Blitztein and an aristocrat to the toenails, had declared years earlier: "*The Cradle Will Rock* is the gayest and most absorbing piece of musical theater that the American Left has inspired. . . . long may it remind us that union cards can be as touchy a point of honor as marriage certificates." Beyond the force of these dynamos, Marc had the added glamour of *one who had been there*—of one now unavailably away in the wars. The music, so ubiquitous in the thirties, was no longer played, but the spirit held firm.

Then suddenly he returned, a hero in uniform, and Lenny premiered, in April of 1945, the ambitious *Airborne Symphony*, with Orson Welles as narrator, eighty male members of Robert Shaw's Collegiate Chorale, and Leo Smit as pianist with the New York City Symphony. Who was I to express a purely artistic dissension among these committed intellectuals? Yet I was appalled. What I intuited then I affirm today: The piece was patriotic smarm. Admittedly I have an allergy to melodrama—to, that is, speech-ified music—unless the verbalism is tightly rhythmicized, as Walton so cannily rhythmicized Sitwell's *Façade*. (If the sung voice is the most musical of instruments, the spoken voice is the least.) Thus masterworks like Debussy's *Martyre,* Stravinsky's *Perséphone,* Honegger's *Jeanne* go against my grain even as I revel in their sonic superstructure and fairly classy texts. But Blitzstein's text for *Airborne* gives new meaning to overstatement, a *Reader's Digest* tribute to our Air Force, preachy, collegiate, unbuttressed, as Copland's corny *Lincoln Portrait* is buttressed, by a less than trite musical background. The few non-embarrassing moments in the score are too close for comfort to *L'Histoire du soldat,* and in the libretto to Whitman's diary. Bernstein was to appropriate Blitzstein's sentimentality—the boyish belief in Man's essential Good—and to use it better. "Better" always meant better tunes.

(Of music's five properties—harmony, counterpoint, rhythm, color, and melody—melody is sovereign; without a sense of contagious melody a composer is not a composer.)

A great work is one you can never get used to. I grew used immediately to the *Airborne Symphony,* which went in one ear and out the other with no trace of residue.

———

That July, after lying fallow during the war, Tanglewood splendidly reopened to a mass of talent unequaled since Paris in the twenties. The student composers, including me, were lodged at a girls' school in Barrington where we gave parties. To one of these Lenny brought his weekend guest, Marc Blitzstein, and we all played our little pieces hoping to impress. Then Marc sat down and sang, one after another, his various hit arias—"Nickel Under the Foot," "Penny Candy," "Zipper Fly"—with such tough and telling charm that, yes, suddenly everything fell together, the pudding was in the eating, the components of his art meshed. Harmony churned, counterpoint spoke, the rhythm was catchy and the color luminous, the tunes came across, all precisely because they spewed from Marc's own body, then lingered like a necessary infection to love. Next morning, if the songs were gone Marc's fragrance remained.

During the fall, as a student at Juilliard where to qualify for a degree one had to take Sociology, I phoned Marc for an interview about his ideas on Art and Society. What do I recall of our talk that November afternoon in the one-room flat at 4 East 12th where he lived until he died? I who felt no relationship with—much less a need for diverting—the masses? I recall that Marc called Poulenc a sissy. That he called Cocteau a *true* artist, while claiming that anyone who could turn a fable of Love and Death into something as "chic" as *L'Éternel retour* (all the rage then in New York), especially by labeling the love potion "poison," was hardly a *great* artist. That all music to him was political. That he looked like Keenan Wynn. That he said, "Admit it, you didn't really come here to interview me for your class."

During the next sixteen years we were friends, even when far away, friends, that is, as much as quasi mentor and reluctant pupil can platonically be. I sense that, while never saying so, Marc always misguidedly felt I was too much the prey of the upper class to write important music. As for the lower class, I never saw that, except for sex, Marc was a mingler there. He liked good food and drink, and shunned the reality of deprivation.

Why, I recently asked a person who knew them both, was Lenny such a devoted admirer of Marc? Because, said the person, Marc was a failure. Well, Lenny worshipped Aaron too, and Aaron was a success? Yes, but Aaron was that much older (b. 1900 as against Marc b. 1905), and a monolithic idol for us all. True, there are cases where two friends, one famous and one not, are switched overnight in the world's eye, as Lenny was switched in rapport with composer Paul Bowles, and later with Marc. Bowles went on to plow (successfully) other fields, while Marc persevered in Lenny's shade. But if Marc could ever have been deemed a failure, he is not that today, and his renaissance, as well as his historicity (he's been gone for nearly two generations), now allows him to be judged in perspective.

———

July 14, 1949
Dear Ned:
Yes, you may use my name as reference for a Guggenheim.
. . . I envy you Paris, and I remember that gone feeling.
Me, I just sit chained to the desk, getting the orchestration
of the new opera done in time for a deadline.
    As ever,
    (signed) Marc Blitzstein

The new opera was *Regina,* his first in twelve years, which was premiered four months later.

November 8, 1957
Dear Ned:
I was charmed and impressed with the tribute, and with the quality of the song. But when you go to the trouble of making a fine piece and dedicating it to me, why the hell don't you present it in person?
  My love.
  Marc

The "tribute" was a setting of Paul Goodman's "Such Beauty As Hurts to Behold," which I felt worthy of Marc. Earlier that year I had written a one-act opera, *The Robbers,* to my own text based on Chaucer's "The Pardoner's Tale." Marc was dismayed—he said I'd got lost in "libretto land" with my arch and archaic locutions. He undertook to rewrite the entire text; without changing a note of the music he refashioned every verbal phrase so that it fell more trippingly on the tongue. This was a voluntary two-day job for which I thanked him with the little song.

Jan. 6, 1959
Dear Ned:
Here is the piece, and a note to Bill Flanagan, which I beg you to deliver. I despair of reaching you by phone; my hours are a mess of disorganization. . . .
  Love,
  Marc

The "piece" was a 500-word essay, "On Two Young Composers," contributed at my prodding to launch a program of songs by me and William Flanagan (whom he'd never met), which took place on February 24. The first general paragraph, beginning

"Songs are a tricky business" (even more apt today than then), is wise, original, and bears reprinting. Of Bill he concludes, "A certain modesty dwells in his music; it should not be confused with smallness." Of me: "Ned Rorem makes thrusts, each of his songs is a kind of adventure. . . . It is a long time since anyone brought off the grand style, outsized sweeping line, thunder and all, that marks 'The Lordly Hudson.' He will one day write an impressive opera. . . ."

> *August 6, 1959*
> Dear Ned:
> It was a glorious trip, from all points of view—including *amours* and the business aspect. And I want to thank you for your letters—although I never got to use the Auric or the Veyron-Lacroix; and Marie-Laure, after a series of *contretemps,* wired me to come see her in Hyères, which I couldn't. . . . I've tried to reach you by 'phone; now [Morris] Golde tells me you are in Wis. I have decided to accept the song-cycle commission from Alice Esty (who tells me your Roethke songs are nearly finished, you dog); and it is in line with that that I write you now. . . . Did you make some kind of deal with Roethke regarding the commission? And if so, what? Do you mind telling me? I want to do the right thing; at the same time I am puzzled as to how to share the commission with the poet (of existing poems), if at all. So do write me here, outlining your procedure in the matter. . . .
> And love,
> Marc

Alice Esty, an adventuresome soprano, commissioned, between 1959 and 1966, three composers a year to write cycles for her, starting with Marc, me, and Virgil T. My cycle was on poems of Theodore Roethke who sent me several lively letters, not at all about esthetics, but setting forth in canny paragraphs exactly what he wanted in residuals, and asking for equal billing on the printed score. (We met only once, not at the concert where the songs were premiered, but at the party afterward, where he showed up, drunk.) I don't know what kind of a "deal" Marc finally made with *his* poet, e. e. cummings, but his group of seven songs, *From Marion's Book,* is, for my metabolism, his very best work. Just as Tennessee Williams's best stories are better than his best plays, precisely because he knows that those stories will never be known by the vast philistine matinee public and can thus be impulsively as convoluted and intimate as he feels, so Marc's concert songs do not, by definition, pander to the big audience. Not that such pandering is in itself wrong; only when an intellectual designs for the hoi polloi. Marc was an intellectual where Lenny Bernstein was not (although he tried to be and was, in fact, smarter than many an intellectual). Lenny, like Poulenc, wrote the same *kind* of music for his sacred as for his profane works; Marc tempered his language according to whom he was addressing.

February 24, 1960
Dear Ned:
A sweet wire, for which I thank you. I feel badly that our rehearsals didn't allow me to get to your concert. . . . I have just come from Carnegie Hall, where Poulenc stubbed his toe flatly in *La Voix humaine.* A comic "camp" is bearable; a serious "camp" is utterly phony.
   Love,
   Marc

June 29, 1960
Dear Ned:
How good to hear from you. The name Yaddo awoke all sorts of fine memories. Do give my warmest to Elizabeth [Ames] and any others who remember me. . . . "Jasager" *is* a beautiful piece. As to copies of the piano-vocal score: I'm sure Lehman Engel must have at least one. He did it way

back in the thirties, with the Henry Street Settlement
chorus, I think; and I seem to remember it was in English. . . .
Incidentally, what about the Brecht estate? They'll raise a
fit if it's known that an "unauthorized" translation has been
made and used, even if non-commercially. Lenya, I have
found to my sorrow, isn't enough when it's a Brecht-Weill
work. . . . I had Shirley Rhoads to my place for a swim yesterday. She is fine, still living (according to her) in a dump,
this time in Lobsterville on the other side of this divine
island. Maybe sometime in August you'd like to come visit
me for a couple of days? Although I warn you I'll be lousy
company; all work and swimming, that's me this summer.
The opera is hard, hard. I do nearly twelve hours a day. I
suppose I'll look back on this period of struggle with love
and envy.

    All affection.

That would have been mailed from Martha's Vineyard to Yaddo.
The opera he speaks of was the uncompleted *Sacco and Vanzetti*.
References to Kurt Weill's *Der Jasager* concerned my project of
producing it at the University of Buffalo. This I eventually did,
with my own translation, and with nobody's permission.

    Two years later it was Marc who was in Yaddo, I in New York. I
planned in February to come to Yaddo, which would have meant
my taking over Marc's room there, but changed my mind, remaining in the city instead to rehearse for another of the American
song concerts Bill Flanagan and I had made into an annual ritual.
From Yaddo, then, came this postcard, the last written communication I had from Marc.

Feb. 22, 1962
Dear Ned:
Thanks for the aviso. I shall probably stay on, as Elizabeth
has asked me to. But I must come into town for some days:

probably around March 18–19. Will you be seeable? Work goes fine, if slowly. I wish I could come to your concert, no soap. I enjoyed the leaflet, but I wish you and Bill would stop those artsy-fartsy *Harper's Bazaar* photos. Still, it's your face, and a beauty too. My love to Bill and you.

    Marc

I have no copies of any letters I may have sent to Marc. But before he left for Martinique I made this entry in my diary:

3 October, 1963. Last night the Rémys came to dine, with Shirley and Marc Blitzstein. Marc gets pugnacious after two drinks, interpreting virtually any remark by anyone as either approbation of or a threat to some dream vision of the Common Man who hasn't existed in thirty years. But the Rémys were bewitched, having never encountered this particular breed of American, probably because Marc is a breed of one, who, like John Latouche in the old days, when on his best behavior, is the most irresistibly quick man in the world.

I never saw him again. Three weeks later he left for Fort-de-France in Martinique, and eleven weeks after that he was dead. On January 22, 1964, a shocked and respectful world received the news, via the *New York Times* front page, announced as an auto accident. Next day the *Times* amended the story. It was learned that he had been set upon by three Portuguese sailors who, with drunken promises of sex, lured him into an alley where they left him moneyless, naked, and battered.

Beyond the horror and dejection, how did I react to Marc's death? With a sort of surprise? He had led, on his special terms, an organized and exemplary life, and was critical of those who hadn't. With me he was avuncular, and vaguely protective esthetically and hygienically: Don't listen to too much Ravel; be sure to do this or that after sex with strangers. This grown-up, this model, *allowed* himself to be murdered? And in midstream. His opera was definitely scheduled for the Met (although Bing is said to have said, "Were Sacco and Vanzetti lovers, like Romeo and Juliet?").

From my diary:

27 January. Except for Bill Flanagan whom I see every day, Marc was the only composer I frequented *as a composer,* someone to compare notes with. When we'd finish a piece we'd show it to each other, as in student days, hoping for praise, getting practical suggestions. Our language, on the face of it, would seem to be the same (diatonic, lyric, simple). In fact, we barked up very different trees. Marc was nothing if not theatrical, and precisely for that he showed me how the element of theater was integral even to remote forms like recital songs.

Malamud is an author whose subject matter (Jewish poverty in Brooklyn) I'd seem to have little in common, but with whose *Assistant* I identified totally. It's discouraging to realize that Marc's best work was his last, *Idiots First,* which he played me just months ago. Malamud would have continued to be his ideal collaborator.

My charm, if I have any, is economized for occasion. Marc's was squandered freely. When as a Juilliard student I first knocked on his door for an interview, Marc Blitzstein received me with a— a sort of Catholic Impatience, worn like a cloak, as he sat at his piano criticizing Cocteau for being fashionable. Have been going through my diary of that period, which talks of the slush in the gutters, Marc's postwar indignations, etc.

I've always felt it, of course, but more and more I've come actually to see that happiness not only precedes but accompanies calamity.

I have just listened, without intermission, to the new CD of Marc's own opera—on Lillian Hellman's *Little Foxes*—*Regina,* all 153 minutes of it. Here are some notes taken during that experience:

I am not a reviewer, I am a composer and a sometime critic; but I do read reviews and see how they shouldn't be done. (Is the reviewer's description of a new work, for example, succinct enough to show whether he likes it without his saying "I like it"? Does he describe the work, or the performance of the work?)

Much has been made about Hellman's continual interference — how she forbade Blitzstein's numerous embellishments on her play. Playwrights, if still alive, can be a thorn in their composers' side (so goes the received opinion); why don't they just shut up? The play, *The Little Foxes*, will survive on its own, and a composer's domain is a separate dimension. During the lifetimes of Blitzstein and Hellman, the opera was never produced as the composer envisioned it. Am I a minority in believing Hellman was right about the musicalizing of her play? The present recording is the first complete recording, and proves that more is less.

When Poulenc expands Bernanos's *Dialogues des Carmélites,* from a filmscript based on Gertrud von Le Fort's German novella, the Bernanos text stays intact, though Poulenc overlays five ritual numbers from Latin liturgy. Four of these serve as prayers-without-action to close scenes; the fifth, the final *Salve Regina,* impels the action when, with each crunch of the guillotine, the music modulates upward, thinning out bit by bit, until all sixteen nuns are dead. These interpolations do not "open up" the story; they intensify a basically motionless drama by entering, as only music can, the mute interior of monastic life. The play is tightened into a necessary opera; there is something to sing about.

When Blitzstein expands a densely plotted story about "the little foxes that spoil the vines," he widely revised, and with the addition of jazz bands, Negro spirituals, party music, "set" numbers on his own doggerel. The play is loosened into an unnecessary extravaganza, because otherwise there would be nothing to sing about. True, certain non-Hellman parts of the piece — such as the "Rain Quartet" and the terrific Dance Suite in Act II — make arguably the best music in *Regina,* just as the Latin choral numbers are the most beautiful parts of *Dialogues;* but where these are extraneous those are integral. Whatever else Hellman's play

may be, it's economical: The power of her craft lies in the claustro-
phobia of greed, her principal characters are hopelessly naughty
and unpoetic. Even without the composer's accessories, it's ques-
tionable whether any opera can depict unalleviated evil. Music,
the most ambiguous of the seven arts, lends sympathy to aberra-
tion. Are not Scarpia, Iago, and Claggart, as repainted by Puccini,
Verdi, and Britten, raised from mere loathsomeness to a sort of
tragic pathos? To hear Regina Giddens and her relatives at song
is to de-fang them; our vines still have tender grapes, and gone is
the hard compulsory shell of Hellman.

Add to this that *Regina* is Blitzstein's only large work not
designed around his own singing voice, using instead the tessi-
turas of operatic professionals as *Porgy and Bess* uses them, and
you have a watery version of the grandiose. Indeed, the tunes and
texture are often pure *Porgy*, but without the seductive guile of
Gershwin's melody. Nor does Marc, with his frequent spoken
interpolations, solve the unsolvable puzzle of how to set pedes-
trian matters to music. The all-northern cast has great fun whoop-
ing it up with southern accents, but their bite is diffused, wilting.
Nor can I seize the sense of some of Marc's text (what does the
much-repeated "Naught's a naught" mean?), while I cringe at
the rhymes ("Greedy girl, what a greedy girl,/Got a greedy guid-
ing star./For a little girl, what a greedy girl you are"), and at the
anachronisms ("A bang-up party, and quaint withal,/to call the
Hubbards the honored guests at their own ball").

This said, something in the sound grows occasionally touching,
echoing a far past, as Monteverdi and Puccini echoed too, except
that this past of Marc's is mine too. It is easy to dub him the poor
man's Kurt Weill in his Common Man works; here lies no trace of
Weill, but Copland rather, laced with Kern, insolently corny and
gorgeously scored. Nor can I deny that I pillaged boldly Birdie's
grand lament about the old homestead, Lionnet, for an aria in my
own *Miss Julie*. The recurrent "dying fall" of a minor third, rising
higher and higher, I owe utterly to Marc.

And I owe to Marc the recurrent motif (also a drooping minor third, this time faster and nasty) in my 1958 orchestral poem, *Eagles*, filched from *his* orchestral poem *Lear*, of the previous year. But this borrowing is of a device (Strauss used it too, in *Salome*), not an esthetic, for Marc did not even superficially influence me.

––––––––

Leftover notes:

Although Lenny Bernstein would never have been quite what he was without the firm example of Marc Blitzstein, there's nothing Marc did that Lenny didn't do better. A like analogy may be drawn between what the giant developer, Aaron Copland, borrowed (and glorified) from the midget pioneer, Virgil Thomson — or between Britten and Holst, Debussy and Rebikov, Wagner and Spohr. The greatest masters are not the greatest innovators. (Picasso: *Je trouve d'abords, je cherche après*.) Marc Blitzstein, oddly, was not even an innovator, except geographically: What Weill stood for in Germany, Marc stood for in America: the sophisticated soi-disant spokesman of the people. His biggest hit was the arrangement of Weill's "Mack the Knife," which infiltrated even *The Fantasticks*.

Marc, the populist, hung out with aristocrats; Poulenc, the aristocrat, hung out with bartenders.

Good reviews don't make me feel as good as bad reviews make me feel bad, but no reviews are worst of all. This sentiment which all artists feel (don't they?) was rejected haughtily by Marc. Yet in 1955 when *Reuben Reuben* (on that hopeless subject: lack of communication) was so roundly loathed by the tryout audiences that they spat upon him, Marc was reduced to tears. Out of context I recall the songs, as he sang them to me, through my own tears. Indeed, so touched was I by the composer's wheezy intoning of "The Very Moment of Love," meant for a chorus in an insane asylum, that he copied it out for me in a little autograph album, which lies before me now. That song, like the songs in *From Marion's Book*, like the "Letter to Emily" in *Airborne*, like Birdie's aria—they stick in the mind.

Yet I am not a fan. I state this advisedly, knowing most of the music pretty well, and giving the man—because he was a friend—the benefit of the doubt (a benefit not accorded to, say, Glass or Carter).

After accepting the invitation to write this little essay (Sandy McClatchy hoped for a straight critique of the new *Regina* recording), I wished I'd refused, but it was too late. Of the fifty-odd essays I've written over the decades about twentieth-century matters musical, just one has been a harsh reaction to the work of a friend: Virgil Thomson. We both lived to rue this. In 1972, after thirty years of mutely despising Thomson's music, and figuring that he, as a major critic who dished it out regularly, wouldn't mind a taste of his own medicine, I presumed finally to voice my feelings in print. Virgil was not thrilled. When he deigned to speak to me five years later, I vowed never again to weaken a friendship by attacking the vital organs. (Contrary to some opinions, it is not pleasant to write unpleasant reviews.) In retrospect, probably it was better for my soul to have said my say and be remorseful than to have stayed mute and be regretful.

With Marc my ambivalence is by definition removed. I loved the man and hated much of the music, hated the man and loved much of the music. He can't defend himself today, but the music can. That music can shout me down. Still, I can live without it. For artistic if not for moral reasons I am unable to discuss it persuasively, and thus should not perhaps have penned these pages. It's too soon to know if my soul is the better for it.

1993

Perceiving Franco

Thirty-three years ago Franco Zeffirelli made his directorial Broadway debut with Dumas's *Lady of the Camellias,* starring a weirdly miscast "method" actress, Susan Strasberg, in a plush adaptation by the young Terrence McNally, and with music by myself. The play folded after four evenings. But in the preceding weeks I had ample time to examine the maestro at work.

Unlike other renowned Jacks-of-all-trades—Cocteau, for example, who wrote the dramas he often produced, or Leonard Bernstein, who composed the music he often conducted—Zeffirelli is not a creator. He is the ultimate re-creator, an interpreter deluxe, responsible for everything about the play except the play itself. With *Camellias,* if he did not write the book, or indeed the music (although at his urging I piped a four-handed version of Weber's *Invitation to the Dance* through an echo chamber), he did design the sets and costumes, affix a viewpoint by relating the tragedy in flashback, and direct the entire goings on. I was awed by his energy, his scope, his sense of detail, his "democracy," and a bit contemptuous (was I jealous?) of his knack for beguiling everyone with his Italianate charm; he would simultaneously supervise the installation of a Louis XV *bergère,* correct the diction (in fluent but accented English) of an understudy, regulate the dynamics

of the tape recorder, even sew on a button while, with a studied
casualness, he fraternized with adoring stagehands.

We were both thirty-nine. But he was (still is) far more famous
than any composer can hope to be. As figures of commerce and
glamour, interpreters today overshadow those they interpret: Tenors and actresses and directors are apotheosized, while authors
and painters are comparatively invisible, with composers at the
bottom of the heap.

His fame preceded him. I am not an opera buff in the sense
of being more taken with singing than with what's sung. For me,
bel canto emphasizes the gargoyles more than the cathedral. Yet
in London, three years earlier, I heard—saw—an unknown Joan
Sutherland, manipulated by Zeffirelli, make sense of Lucia's mad
scene by cupping her hand to her ear, heeding her alter ego as
echoed by the schizophrenic flute. The young Callas too, launched
by Visconti and later given a second, brief life by Zeffirelli, lent new
meaning to Italian song, and changed forever the way the world
responds to all opera, including American opera. Samuel Barber,
who devised *Vanessa* for her, was devastated when she turned it
down. She was never to sing in English, her native tongue. Nor did
Zeffirelli, so far as I know, ever direct an opera in English, except
for Barber's *Anthony and Cleopatra,* which opened the new Met
in 1966. The director inadvertently subverted the score, which he
considered chamber music, by introducing live mammals—were
they camels?—amidst the supernumeraries, and a giant sphinx
on a turntable, which collapsed mid-performance.

However, following the 1963 failure of *Camellias* (after which
I would not see him for another three decades), he did direct a
series of English-language movies, mostly Shakespeare, with a
care for verse and visual nuance which perhaps only a foreigner
can impose. His *Romeo and Juliet* (1968) is a Renaissance painting in motion, every frame a masterpiece in itself, even as it serves
the ongoing whole. The music (by Nino Rota), mostly in slow or
fast waltz time, and the speech, mostly in iambic pentameter,

combine in a continual counterpointing of three against five, delicious to my American ear. His *Hamlet* (1990), with the successfully perverse casting of Mel Gibson as star, is witty and poignant in its treatment of language, virile and melancholy in its view of Danish royalty in decay.

If the Barber opera was an expensive dud, Zeffirelli two years earlier had made a joint debut with Bernstein at the old Met, in a production of *Falstaff,* resulting in one of the happiest collaborations in Met history. The two men were profoundly similar, profoundly different. Each seemed flamboyantly self-involved and flamboyantly generous, each held an extravagant vision of artistic presentation yet with tight control, and each concurred, in his own Mediterranean manner, on the approach to British whimsy. Viewed from outside, their ascending careers had also been similar: Each was internationally celebrated, highly paid, and in constant demand, yet treated grudgingly, even sarcastically, by the press, at least on this side of the Atlantic, until well into middle life. But politically they were on opposite sides. Bernstein, forever left-wing, lent his name and his gifts to every imaginable radical cause. Zeffirelli, forever right-wing, even campaigned for the Senate of the new party in Sicily, Forza Italia. (In a recent *New Yorker* profile he declared "that he would impose the death penalty on women who had abortions.")

If LB was progressive in championing new music, his own and hundreds of others', FZ's conviction in matters artistic is literally to conserve. What contemporary works has he directed? Eduardo de Filippo certainly, two Albee plays, I believe, and a filmed remake of *The Champ*. But no Gershwin or Berg, no Beckett or Brecht, no studies of the downtrodden, like those of his chief mentor, Luchino Visconti. "These new operas!" he has said. "It is a left-wing plot. . . . I am a totally understood artist. I am misunderstood only by the left wing, who expect me to do something different every time." Yes, he centers on the tried-and-true with his personal focus for Shakespeare, Puccini, Da Ponte, Mérimée, Verdi.

Other stylish directors are equally reactionary, but hide behind specious "relevance," updating everything except the music (why *not* the music?), while Zeffirelli simply makes a work more of what it already is. "You must be faithful to the author," says he. His aim is "to take the audience by the hand and make them revisit a lost planet. We cry and laugh for the same reasons the ancient Egyptians or nineteenth-century Romans cried and laughed. The passions of the human heart never change."

"Taste" and "opulence" are the nouns most often cited for his effect, though the nouns are in some way mutually exclusive, the one implying restraint, the other excess. It will be intriguing to note how these traits color his imminent mounting of *Carmen* at the Met. To this end the *New York Times* asked me to draw him out.

———

A few weeks ago we spoke, I in Nantucket and he in Positano, for the first time in decades. I was touched by his warm use of the second person singular, his constant interpolations of "luv" and "caro," his patience with my rusty stabs at his language ("You need to get an Italian lover," he suggested), and his eagerness at my invitation to dine on the evening of his arrival in New York. "But only if I do the cooking," he insisted. "I'll bring a special tomato sauce on the plane. All you need do is get the pasta which is so marvelous over there." Well, Americans mean what they say though they don't always say what they mean, while Italians always say what they mean, but don't always mean what they say. Will he not show up? Or show up with an entourage, but not bring the sauce?

When I brought up *Carmen* he grew serious, if not especially informative. "I've already staged it three times. This time will be the barest, the strangest." Will he stage the overture in flashback, as he did in the film of *La Traviata*? "Er . . . Each of the four preludes is a jewel, announcing without words the dire consequences of the scenes to follow. Carmen can *read* destiny. Which is why she plays cards. But *gypsy* cards." Dare I ask how he plans to restrict the freest of all operatic souls — he who speaks against women's freedom of choice?

If a new version of *Carmen* is hardly earth-shattering as compared to, say, a new Italian opera, anything by Franco is, at the least, news, and at the most a massive frisson.

––––––––

Franco Zeffirelli arrives alone, but with enough fettucine to feed a regiment, though we will be only four. Also are plastic bags of sauce, one a sausage and spice mixture, another of basil and tomatoes just plucked from his garden in Positano. This fare he has toted from Rome, with a stopover in London, landing in New York last night. Today he has spent conferring at the Met. Tomorrow he will fly to Los Angeles to stage *Pagliacci* for Domingo, thence to Tokyo for a new production of *Aida* before returning here to rehearse for the October 31 opening of *Carmen*. Meanwhile, indefatigable, he immediately asks for the kitchen, where for the next hour he will chop and stir and sample, while downing a stiff Scotch on the rocks (he will also down a bottle of Campaccio, assuring us "I've never been drunk in my life"), and commuting to the parlour where he does a quick imitation of Sutherland as Lucia trying to appear two feet shorter, at his direction, by squatting beneath her capacious skirt. Then back to the stove without missing a beat of the monologue about his two most compelling loves, Callas and Visconti: how the former's spirit was broken during her Onassis years; how the latter allowed him — Franco — to be held by the police relating to a robbery of which he was clearly innocent; yet how both were among the magic few of the true gods he has known. Indeed, he is now mulling a filmscript dealing with the unknown final month of the diva's life.

Franco is not onstage, playing the lofty star. He's been everywhere and knows everyone and is in fact a star himself, but like all stars he's also star-struck, like we lesser mortals. He does know his worth, makes his points succinctly, sometimes as if by rote. Nervous, voluble, disheveled, he remains handsome with a confidential twinkle of youth, has an appealing tic around the mouth, and chain smokes needle-thin Superleggeras, which he puts out in his undrunk espresso.

While grating the parmesan he explains that, of his triple-threat professions, opera and theater and film, opera is where his lasting contribution lies. He can afford this contribution because of the vast success of his Shakespeare movies wherein he has reintroduced high culture not only to England but to receptive young innocents around the globe. Yes, movies are bigger than life, from outside in, by virtue of the medium, but opera is bigger than life from the inside out. He doesn't particularly aim for grandiosity, it just comes out that way as the nature of the beast.

As for straight plays, maybe he is least at home there, as witness the Dumas drama which he has directed in all three mediums, most persuasively as *La Traviata*. What he wants with opera is to intensify, not change.

Hearing him on opera one suspects that music is but one of the form's various components, that apparel and scenery and choreography are every bit as crucial. Does he read music? No. But orchestral rehearsals without the singers are revelations: instrumental sonority corresponds to a cinematic close-up, and the fact that an oboe and not a horn is featured here or there necessarily sways his view, if only subliminally, on how an actor will move.

What about speech patterns? Does Italian have an inherent verse rhythm, as French has alexandrines and English has iambic pentameter, which necessarily affect even a nation's non-vocal music? Is Dante's *terza rima* based on indigenous phonetics? Franco is not interested. Anyway, we're about to sit down.

(Pasta like velvet, sauce like ambergris, etc., plus casaba melon, green salad, fudge cake with whipped cream, enough red wine.) We touch on Carmen, a true working-class heroine. Will his treatment of her behavior, her stance, her very singing, differ from, say,

Tosca's, though both are in a sense actresses? No, because each is bigger than life, an individual, and thus uncategorizable, and yes, for the same reason. Remember: Carmen is the first, and only, totally free female spirit in all opera. (Even, I wonder, to arranging her own suicide by execution?)

Will this, his fourth mounting of the opera, differ from the others? Like me, does he feel that his old pieces need to move ever faster with every passing year? Yes, because we are both growing older.

Has he seen *Carmen Jones*? "Yes, it's the best treatment so far!"

Perhaps Franco's *Carmen* lies more in the doing than the telling. With a tinge of mischief I offer him my long essay on the subject written seventeen summers ago. "*O Dio,*" he sighs. "Now I suppose I'll have to change my whole approach." But when he peeks at the last sentence—"*Carmen* is great, but Bizet is not"—he looks reproachful. Clearly he is convinced that whatever masterpiece he embellishes *is* a masterpiece. Most of these masterpieces are nineteenth century, and hence, at least to American ears, romantic. Yet at the hint that his tastes are romantic he bristles. Perhaps the word has another connotation to Latins. "How can you say that *Who's Afraid of Virginia Woolf?* [which he triumphantly directed in both French and Italian] is romantic?" he pleads, though how else to classify a work wherein a married couple, for three hours, rant and cajole and finally weep about their beloved fantasy child? If not a romantic, how else characterize a man of such obvious intelligence, who yet shuns any form of theater not driven by gripping plot propelled by emotions on the verge of self-destruction?

He may well empathize with modern American theater, having directed, in translation, besides the Albee plays, productions of Steinbeck and Tennessee Williams, and filmed two "realistic" American soapers, *The Champ* (Faye Dunaway) and *Endless Love* (Brooke Shields), but his disinterest in American opera is resounding. Unaware of both *Four Saints in Three Acts* and *Nixon in China,* he nonetheless disqualifies them *in absentia* because "they are not in the repertory." When he ponders why neither *Wuthering Heights* nor *Streetcar* has ever been musicalized, I tell him how Carlisle Floyd composed a viable setting of the Bronte in 1958, and how John Harbison is currently working on the Williams. Hmmm, says Franco, toying with his necklace of gold amulets, gifts from the great, a blessed medal from the Pope, for example, and the *lettera aleph* from Bernstein. "Ah, Lenny, Lenny, how I miss him. *He's* the one who would have written the great American opera."

Nor does Britten tempt him (*"Peter Grimes* works only because of the strong libretto"), nor Poulenc. Still, it would be fun to see how he might deal with wild farce like Poulenc's *Les Mamelles,* or, on a bare stage, how he might treat a vast tragedy like Stravinsky's *Oedipus Rex.* Even a play by Genet or Cocteau. But no. As for Germans, again no, despite his first childhood exposure to opera being through *Die Walküre,* which bedazzled him. He *would* like to film Berg's *Lulu* someday, if he could use Stratas, which seems unlikely, and if he knew German, which he doesn't. However, his new Carmen, Waltrud Meier, is German.

Next month, since music is a universal language (as the silly saying goes), this truism will again be proved when our Italian directs the French opera about a Spanish gypsy sung by a German with a Mexican co-star, under an American conductor.

———

Around midnight as he is leaving, Franco hands me a video. This turns out to be his induction into, and his convocational address to the valedictorians at, the University of Kent in Canterbury Cathedral last month. His theme is commendably predictable (the riddle of how art can save an increasingly artless society) and his words are standard ("You kids are about to enter a cruel world"). But his mien is eloquent beyond words, as he stands there like a

wistful boy in tasseled hat and flowing robes. As with his beloved
Lenny, one is now struck by how the Zeffirellian force stems not
from diction but from action, not rhetoric but physical example,
not intellect but instinct. Like all artists, no matter how glorious
("Beauty is but a flower/Which wrinkles will devour"), he seems
vulnerable, even insecure, anxious for all of us to love and admire
not only his hard work but his very being.

1996

Morton Gould

When we were adolescents in Chicago, my sister Rosemary and I thought it would be nice to become dancers when we grew up. To this end we choreographed a duet to a Glenn Miller record called "Pavane" and performed it for anyone who'd watch. As I stand here, fifty-seven years later, I can still feel that music's kinetic force; it had everything: contagious rhythm, piquant harmony, seductive scoring, a sense of direction, and, above all, a good tune. Its composer was—according to a minute parentheses beneath the title on the ten-inch disc—someone named Morton Gould. MOR-TON-GOULD. Those three dark syllables rolled on the tongue like chocolate, but who was the man behind them? How could I know that someday we would become staunch colleagues? You just don't *meet* idols—for when you do, they cease being idols and turn into vulnerable flesh, like you and me.

While I was jitterbugging in the Midwest, Morton Gould, ten years my senior, was already, at twenty-four, the chief composer and conductor for Manhattan's station WOR. It was the Golden Age of Radio, and Morton arranged weekly national broadcasts of classical music, including his own. He had already been a professional for ten years as a piano prodigy whose recitals were partly devoted to improvisations on themes given by the audience. By 1943 he had composed the keyboard *Concertette*, which would be transformed by Jerome Robbins two years later as the ballet *Interplay*. By the decade's end he had written the Broadway musical *Billion Dollar Baby* with Comden and Green, the dance drama *Fall River Legend* with Agnes DeMille, and three film scores, including *Delightfully Dangerous* starring Jane Powell. In 1966, he conducted an all-Ives recording with the Chicago Symphony, which won a Grammy.

During the next thirty years he grew ever more prolific, composing for radio, Broadway, ballet, Hollywood movies, documentaries, and television, as well as band, chorus, and orchestra works of every stripe, concocting sounds that were unmistakably American in their use of the jazz that was his very marrow. Witness the witty *Tap Dance Concerto* of 1952, and the very recent *Rap Concerto*. Lots of young Americans speak proprietarily of the new Crossover Music, music which more or less blends pop with classical. Wasn't this process simply called Third Stream a generation ago? In fact, hasn't it been around since Gottschalk 150 years ago? By the twenties it had become serious business, with Carpenter and Copland, Grofé and Blitzstein, when the young Morton Gould emerged from their luminous wake. If Gould lacked the infectious melodiousness of Gershwin or the salubrious vulgarity of Bernstein playing the same game, he was equally immediate, and perhaps more versatile than either. For he was simultaneously active as educator, as conductor, *and* as official in the tough job of distribution, notably as director of ASCAP where for eight years he kept symphonic music's head above water, while promoting pop icons in their various guises.

Like the four other artists evoked today, Morton is a leaf fallen from our family tree, and the world's weight seems sadly lighter. Nor will the leaf ever grow back: every work of art, unlike an automobile or a violin, is unique and irreplaceable. The French movie director Jean-Pierre Melville, when asked to state his ultimate goal, replied: "To become immortal, and then to die." The first half of that goal has, by definition, been reached by every Academy member in this room. But for Morton the goal is particularly poignant by virtue of his age. Unlike a Sibelius or a Rossini who burned out early, Morton was still fertile as a rabbit when at age seventy-seven he joined the Academy, eighty when he received a Kennedy Center Award from Clinton, eighty-one when only last year he got the Pulitzer Prize for what was the strongest piece of his career, the thirty-minute *String Music,* and eighty-two when he passed away last March in Orlando, presumably happy, prior to a concert he was to conduct at a three-day festival honoring his work.

No music, certainly no non-vocal music, can be proved to have literary or visual reference, and such scores as purport to extra-musical intent usually depict nothing less vague than water or love or funerals. Still, it's fun to ascribe metabolic natures to composers, like Strauss and Mahler, say, or Ravel and Debussy, as flip sides of the coin of optimism and pessimism. Morton was decidedly optimist. Even such works as the 1947 ballet on Lizzie Borden, or the 1978 *Holocaust Suite,* though formidably theatrical, are never morbid. Likewise his personality.

I didn't know him very well; I was never in his house, nor he in mine. Though if to "know well" deals with intensity rather than frequency, we were intimates. The very tie that now adorns my neck was bestowed by his beloved Claire. He was a good talker. If his music was always, to use his term, in the vernacular, so was the sound of his New York speech. Like many (though not all) good talkers, he was a good listener. It was hard to break off a conversation; like a child not wanting to go to bed, he would prod each ramification of even the simplest idea. For, yes, despite his informed shrewdness in dealing with the complexities of the commercial music world, he was, like all artists, a child, eager, refusing to call it a day. He died in the middle of a sentence.

For the Academy   *7 November 1996*

Random Notes for a Sketch of Allen

This morning I've been rereading Allen Ginsberg's early poems. Despite their unflagging energy, long lists of Whitmanesque "yawps," all-embracing compassion, and stinging eroticism, I'm impressed anew at how melancholy they mostly seem. Listen:

> . . . all movement stops
> & I walk in the timeless sadness of existence . . .
> my own face streaked with tears in the mirror
>   of some window—at dusk—
>   where I have no desire

Listen:

> . . . this graveyard
> this stillness
>   on deathbed or mountain
> once seen
>   never regained or desired
>   in the mind to come
> where all Manhattan that I've seen must disappear.

Or listen again to the notorious opening of *Howl*:

I saw the best minds of my generation destroyed by madness
       starving hysterical naked
dragging themselves through the negro streets at dawn
                                 looking
    for an angry fix . . .

— followed by a thousand lines of depressing fervor that established Ginsberg, at twenty-nine in 1955, as our most influential
American bard.

The verses recall my own mother, who spent her life as an activ-
ist for pacifism and for all civil rights. When the world did not
listen, she gave up and died. Ginsberg never gave up. Yet with the
years he became less and less the subjective poet and more and
more the objective sloganeer for the teenage minds of the '60s
and '70s: mantras, flower power, LSD, counterculture. But he was
also crucial to more worldly movements: gay rights, environmen-
tal protest, Buddhist solutions to violence. Like Hemingway, he
grew to be more guru than creator.

———

Though close, we never touched, being reverse sides of one coin.
If the whole coin depicted public avowal of homosexuality in a
pre-Stonewall era when people didn't say such things, his side portrayed the magnanimous redskin, mine the paleface narcissist.

Was it in 1958 that we first met? I recall a drunken bunch of us
piling into a cab, lurching from Virgil Thomson's at the Chelsea
to Kenneth Koch's on Perry Street, with me seated happily on his
boyfriend's lap. Did Allen mind? "Not if Peter doesn't," said he,
and began to sing: "Where is the world we roved, Ned Bunn? . . .
who roamed a world young lads no more shall roam." For the next
four decades, whenever he saw me, my name would spark those
verses of Melville. During those same decades two aspects of my
first impression stuck: 1) Allen was as generous *with* his lovers as
he was *to* his lovers; possessive love contradicts all-encompassing

love. 2) Any occasion was occasion for song, song being poetry's primal utterance.

———————

Cut to Tangier in 1961, when this long sentence appears in my diary on August 28:

> Allen Ginsberg, who breakfasts on éclairs in the Socco Chico, who inhabits a shack-penthouse at the Hotel Armor with Gregory Corso, who takes strong pills with William Burroughs (*Naked Lunch* has power not through order but through accumulation only), and who announced "all" to the *New York Post* two years ago, in short the original obstreperous Beatnick, tells me middle-classedly to "hush" when I ask Paul, in the Mahruba restaurant too loudly before other diners, if the dancing boy is queer.

The "all," uttered to a leering reporter, had been: "Yes, I'm queer as a two-dollar bill." Then why the pious reaction to my question about the dancing boy, since in any case the other diners didn't speak English? As to Burroughs, I found him then as I find him now, a sophomoric bore as a writer, and an unmusically surly lump as a man.

———————

In 1966 were published the confessional *Five Years* of Paul Goodman, and my *Paris Diary*. With Allen Ginsberg we became America's three unapologetic queers. (France for years had Gide and Genet, Cocteau and Montherlant, even as Greece had Cavafy.) Yes, America has always had her outspoken "dirty" authors, but they inevitably wrote in the third person.

———————

The difference as guru between Allen Ginsberg and Paul Goodman is that one catered to the feelings of the young while the other catered to their minds. Obviously Ginsberg won out.

_____

Diary, 1973

One musician's heart sinks on witnessing Allen Ginsberg, presumably oblivious to the TV camera yet mugging like Dean
Martin in slow motion, embedded among acolytes intoning with
mindless de-energized redundant unison the stanzas of William
Blake. Ginsberg acknowledges he's never studied music, that
his settings of Blake are "in a C chord, C-major" (he means in
a non-modulating Ionian mode; his tonic is actually B-flat), and
that he teaches Blake by singing him "because Blake sang, you
know—he was a literal poet."

Formal study would not make Ginsberg a better composer, only
a discerning one. He needs more of an ear; his music may be fun
to join in, as any college songs are for the tone-deaf, but it sounds
colorless, uncommunicative, and wrong for Blake, who needs a
rainbow blaze. To counter, as Ginsberg does, that "nobody knows
what Blake's own music was like, since it was not written down,
but that it was probably similar to what I'm doing . . . [which] is
sort of in the style of Isaac Watts" (a hymnodist who died ten years
before Blake was born), is not only to strain the credulity of his students, but also to *know* the past, and to assume that an ugly drone
is as valid as the simplicities being droned. Even if we did know
Blake's own settings, why set his poems now in the manner of his
time rather than ours? Would rock music embellish these poems?
Maybe, but rock has its own words.

Couldn't Ginsberg musicalize his own good verses instead?
Of course, then he'd risk the inadvertent masochism of a Paul
Goodman, whose non-professional love for music leads him to
believe he's a composer. (Though unlike Pound, who turned to
Villon—as Ginsberg turns to Blake—Paul sabotages his own per-
fect poetry.)

2 March 1974

Tomorrow in Kansas, premiere of *In Time of Pestilence*, six short
madrigals on verses of Thomas Nashe. The choice of poetry for

these a cappella morsels I owe directly to Allen Ginsberg, although he doesn't know it. During an interview with *Gay Sunshine* long ago, Ginsberg quoted the line composed in 1593: "Brightness falls from the air"; and this urged forth my song. Thank you, Allen. Coincidence is not the word for fine minds functioning together while miles apart; it is the word for mediocre minds finding greatness—which is never. There is no coincidence. So I was not surprised to recall the phrase only last night, isolated painfully, as I reread *A Portrait of the Artist* after thirty years. "Brightness falls from the air." Stephen Dedalus recalls the words as he picks a louse from his neck, crushes it between his fingers, and lets it drop shining to the ground.

From the hamlet garden we plaintively watch trains go by. From the train window we enviously see hamlet gardens. Finally enclosed in the actual arms of the butcher we've dreamed about, we dream about the butcher. Go up in flames, go down in flames.

Over the years Allen and I corresponded regularly, if not copiously. We "spoke" solely of poetry as it obtains to music, and as its subject is gay (though neither of us used that word). I was cranky, he was patient. He never raised his voice. Saints don't raise their voices, they inform through example. Still, saints are a dime a dozen, and never really change the world, while poets are rare as rubies and leave us in another dimension.

I prefer to remember Allen as a poet. As such he was—is— dangerous, because his style, conversational and direct (like that of Frank O'Hara, who also at his death spawned mediocre imitators), seems deceptively simple, thus easy to mimic. Still, if there are a thousand faux Ginsbergs about, better that than a thousand Mother Teresas whose pieties have strings attached.

If Allen grew to be less the dreamer and more the rebel, he nonetheless, in 1973, accepted membership to the American Academy of Arts and Letters at whose conformingly prestigious

dinner parties he ambled from table to table photographing fellow members. (These included, after 1983, thanks to Allen's prodding, the non-conformist Burroughs.) It was at the Academy that
I most frequently ran into him, and it was with him I felt most at
ease gossiping about who "was" and who "wasn't" amongst the
distinguished immortals. For after a certain age, the age at which
they become professionals in a competing society, artists together
don't talk about art, they talk shop. Shop means fees, sex, and
death, in that order.

Now I am seventy-four, and thirty-two months older than Allen,
who is gone forever. Thus he enters the realm of those who can
no longer be talked to, but only talked about. And thus what one
says, or at least what I myself feel, is clothed in the haze of hindsight which dispels reservation.

Like all true artists he was one of a kind. The "kind" was bardic,
didactic, personal, where the artist's presence is as crucial as his
work. No one was better at this than Allen Ginsberg. One may
hope that the best of what he has to say, despite his absence from
our fickle society, will last forever.

1997

Louise Talma

Sifting through our occasional correspondence, about concerts of mutual friends, about the trials of latter-day Fontainebleau, about the death of my father whom she never knew, I fall upon these words: "In the lonely quest for notes it helps to know that one's colleagues think well of what one is doing. I am particularly grateful for your last paragraph which sets the record straight. I'm heartily sick of being on programs just because I'm a woman. The work is the only thing that counts."

I had thought it might be stylish to write this epitaph without mentioning that Louise Talma was a woman. But the fact is crucial. As of today there remain, among forty-five men, only three female musicians in this Academy, where Louise, as late as 1974, became the first woman composer. Thirty years earlier she was the first woman composer to receive a Guggenheim. Yet another first came in the mid-1950s when Thornton Wilder, after turning a deaf ear to many a male petitioner, including Aaron Copland, agreed to collaborate with Louise. Her passion for that writer, equaled only by her attachment to her mother, with whom she lived all her life, was requited in an opera, *The Alcestiad*. Premiered in Frankfurt in 1962, the work was the first by an American woman to be produced in a European opera house.

Musical composition is the one art in which, until lately, women have not shone. The reason is not mysterious. Writing notes, with its attendant chores of copying, orchestration, and the cajoling of the mostly male entrepreneurs who might bring these notes to life, simply takes more time away from child-rearing than, say, writing poems. Today there are perhaps as many women as men composers. But in today's world—even in the elite intellectual world of this very Academy—few give a damn. It's safe to say that indifference to female composers is no more evident than to males.

American, born in France in 1906, Louise while still a teenager fell under the spell of our century's most persuasive pedagogue, Nadia Boulanger, a spell that for the rest of her days stamped not only her rigorous technique and emotionally controlled expression, but physical posture, wardrobe, and hairstyle.

The first time I saw her was fifty-two years ago, in the vast rehearsal room of the old City Center, where offbeat concerts were held. She strode onto the platform in a no-frills black gown, didn't bow, sat quickly at the keyboard, and, without missing a beat, slammed into her Toccata, which brought down the house.

The last time I saw her was one year ago. We sat together to hear our pieces at a choral concert and said pleasant things to each other. Always abrasive, Louise at ninety now seemed frail and far away, while straining to keep hold. Her every allusion was musical. But her lack of small talk had always belied her *crafted* talk, and the nature of her music, which was witty, ironic, touching, sometimes heroic, often gorgeous, always healthy and heart-on-sleeve, as in her *Terre de France* on verse of Péguy.

Two months later when Russell Oberlin phoned to say that Louise had left us the night before, during her sleep at her beloved Yaddo (in the very bed where I, too, and many another solitary composer, once wrestled with insomniac dreams), I was moved to consider the intervening half-century.

Claudette Colbert, who died the same day at the same age, had something in common with Louise by being the last of a breed. Louise's breed, profoundly feminine in impulse, was of the willful musician made flesh. Women in the 1930s, no doubt to prove their equality, could write music far more aggressive than their counterparts, those men who meanwhile compose sheer languor, having nothing extra-musical to prove. If Louise was a torch-carrier for Boulanger and the French tradition, she was also the real thing as an individual. (By French tradition I mean vulnerable leanness, with all tones exposed, and a way of turning the quotidian into magic.) We musicalized many of the same poets, notably Dickinson and Hopkins and Cummings and Auden; for me to say that her versions were as valid as mine is to say everything. Maybe the biggest compliment any composer can pay another is one of affinity: You did just what I would have done, if I'd been canny enough to think of it.

Suddenly she has become our vanished sibling, but with the consolation—I *think* it's a consolation—that she will continue to communicate in a thousand shifting forms. It is all very well to say that Louise Talma was second to none in her ability to make a piece go. What counts, as with everyone here, is not her virtuosity, but her involuntary knack for making her works bleed and breathe. At her best, she gave off a sense of necessity, the one ingredient an artist cannot guarantee, but without which no art is art.

For the Academy   *8 April 1997*

re: Glenn Gould

Dear Jennifer Howard—

You will never forgive me, but I can't do the review of the Glenn Gould biography. I'm going through a difficult personal period, and find it difficult to concentrate on what doesn't interest me. Believe me, I've spent a hundred hours reading the book, and making notes. But the writing of Peter Ostwald is lifeless, and numbingly redundant.

The book should appeal to the current childish reader who likes his artists crazy rather than true. Glenn Gould was perhaps both; but, as I explain in the few loosely written paragraphs herewith enclosed, I, as a composer, am not awfully sympathetic with the tribulations of performers. The music with which Gould is linked did not come from him, it came from Bach, from Beethoven, et al. GG is merely the vessel through which their "genius" flowed.

The author, a psychiatrist, though caring and informed musically, is inclined to explain everything with psychobabble. And if he is repetitious, well maybe *all* lives are repetitious. But virtually nothing is revealed about GG's personal life. (In my pages on his affair with a composer's wife, I say more in two sentences than Ostwald in his whole long book.) Apparently GG had no friends, only sycophants, doctors, and business associates who were summarily

thrown out when their usefulness waned. Only his mother—
his beloved mother—remained.

Oh well, forgive me if you can.

And give Marie Arana Ward my love.

Notes Around Glenn Gould

The one time I met Glenn Gould I offered my hand and he recoiled
in horror. That was the autumn of 1960, backstage at a Buffalo
Philharmonic concert on which we both were featured. His reaction seemed less offensive than amusing; already at twenty-eight
Gould was known not only as a keyboard phenomenon but as an
eccentric, shunning tactile exchange with other humans. Soon
after, I nevertheless quizzed a female acquaintance. She, the
wife of a composer-friend, had lived with Gould for two years in
Toronto. How *was* he—I mean sentimentally—I wondered? She
assured me he was loving, considerate, and yes, *tactile*.

Except for that Buffalo concert, when Josef Krips conducted
the Emperor Concerto, I never heard him perform live, though
I did listen with astonishment to his many recordings where, as
critics put it, he played Brahms like Bach, and Bach like Brahms,
meaning that Brahms was contrapuntalized and Bach romanti-
cized. But he never really preoccupied me; my musical needs
lie elsewhere. Still, twenty-two years later I felt the shock of his
early death, announced over my kitchen radio in October 1982:
Another true artist has been stolen from our increasingly mediocre globe. And it was touching to learn that he bequeathed his
estate of nearly a million dollars to the Salvation Army and the
Toronto Humane Society; he had long hoped to found a retire-
ment home for old cows, horses, dogs, and other animals.

———

At the time of his death Gould had become internationally famous,
no less for his hypochondriacal behavior than for his idiosyncratic

pianism, which, since his retiring from the stage in 1964, occurred solely in recording studios, where he would edit as many as fifty splices for one Bach fugue.

Glenn Gould was the thinking man's David Helfgott. Indeed, the publishers of this biography may well profit from the reflected glory of the current movie *Shine*. The author is Peter Ostwald, a psychiatrist and amateur violinist, who died just after completing the book. In a twenty-line blurb on the back of the galleys the word "genius" is dropped seven times, "madness" thrice, and "brilliant"—an adjective so overused as to be meaningless—twice. Even the biographer's widow, in a smarmy foreword, tells of the "immense creative energy" driving him to complete the book before he died: ". . . he would suffer, but the work would not." Amidst this *Shine*-type hype the question is posed: "Do men and women of genius sacrifice themselves for a higher ideal while remaining personally unfulfilled?"

The answer is No. Unfulfilled how? Successfully creative people are the sole beings on earth who know what they want to do, know how to do it, and are appreciated for doing it. But how is "creative" defined? The term is used as ubiquitously for the interpreter as for the maker of music. The usage is common in our century when the living performer is deified, while the living composer is all but invisible; when a superstar tenor can earn in one evening what a composer earns to write a whole opera. Now, since the living performer specializes almost exclusively in the music of the dead, yet since he is also called a creator while playing, say, Mozart, then what is Mozart? Wouldn't it be clearer to define the executant's profession as "re-creator"?

—————

Given these biases, I am perhaps an odd choice to review a book about a famous pianist. Two other biases mitigate against the choice:

Seventeen years ago I began an essay thus: "I am my ideal pianist.

If I'd rather hear myself play than anyone, it's not because I'm better than anyone (there is no 'better than'); it's that my fancy fills in missed notes, the inner ear camouflages mere sloppiness. I play just well enough for perfection, while virtuosos play too well for perfection. Most great pianists perform the same repertory. They can't all be right. But I am right for me. Perhaps the gambit should read: The only pianist for my idealized performance is me."

The other bias, more personal, is that my cultural leanings are French while Gould's are German. (It could be argued—quite Frenchly—that the universe is divided between two esthetics, French and German, and that everyone, including every *thing*, falls into one or the other category.) Ninety percent of the book's musical references are to standard Germanic classics; the only mention of French music, even Debussy's, is sneering or indifferent. (Francis Poulenc's Christian name is even misspelled François.) Almost the only contemporary music Gould played was Schoenberg, whom he worshipped. I am constitutionally incapable of dealing intelligently, much less caringly, with this repertory.

––––––––

Glenn Gould's own prose writing has everything—wit, insight, originality, healthy philistinism, clarity of expression—except warmth, the warmth one finds in those intellectuals he emulates, like Charles Rosen and (sometimes) Robert Craft. And his distancing of himself from what he terms "French impressionists" does make me wistful about how he might have played, say, Ravel. French music needs objectivity, not "feeling." One doesn't always perform best what one loves best; the ego hovers between the keyboard and the composer.

(This letter was never acknowledged.)

Washington Post Book World   *11 May 1997*

Composition Today

This year marks the seventy-fifth birthday not only of WNYC, but of myself. It also marks the fifty-fifth anniversary of my first radio broadcast, which took place in these very studios.

It was February 1944, the Fifth American Music Festival, a series of broadcasts by living composers that would occur annually ever after, between Lincoln's and Washington's birthdays. I still have the little flyer, which my friend Morris Golde printed up, announcing my own half-hour program.

So what has changed by the end of our century? Well, nothing and everything. Nothing, at least insofar as WNYC is concerned. Our city station has had its ups and downs, but the promotion of live American music still obtains, through the yearly celebration and through interviews.

Yet the substance of radio music everywhere now seems to be 99 percent pop versus 1 percent classical, and the little remaining classical is 99 percent nineteenth century and 1 percent twentieth century. The audience for this is not only ignorant adolescents, but cultured adults. Which leaves me and my composing brethren out in the cold. There is scarcely any outlet for contemporary classical music, certainly not on television, which has largely replaced radio.

Let's define terms. "Classical" really refers to a period in history.

It emerged after millennia of mainly church music, thrived in the court during the eighteenth century, was nudged into concert halls by the Romantic movement in the nineteenth century, and by so-called modernism in the twentieth. The current comprehensive title still remains "classical," and is distinguished from pop by being invariable, designed for trained artists, and notated in complex forms. Popular music is generally for untrained performers, variable in all senses, not written down, in tight forms, and almost exclusively vocal.

Pop music, essentially a music of "the people," might be identified as always having the mindless insistence of a steady beat (it keeps workers working), as distinct from the meandering melisma of the cathedral or the "sophisticated" rhythms of the court.

Today, for the first time ever, pop dominates the globe, culturally and financially. In the past five years the situation has worsened. There are fewer than 100 paid classical music critics in the United States; most respectable periodicals have dispensed with them, while retaining pop critics. As for contemporary classical music, it's all but disappeared in the ken of every class. Intellectuals may know all about the other arts, from Giotto to Jackson Pollock, Dante to Philip Roth. But when it comes to music they stop at Verdi and have no concept of living music, except pop. Yet ironically there are more young, serious, *classical* composers around than ever before, really thousands, as opposed to the dozen or so when I was a kid. What's to become of them?

My advice to the young composer is this: Since big orchestras and publishers and record distributors don't want you, stay in school as long as you can and stay chummy with those performers who will otherwise forget you when you're out in the unreal world; start your own small publishing and recording companies; and organize your own small touring ensembles, as Benjamin Britten did in England.

What, then, is the future of classical music? people always ask us older composers, as though we'd know better than they. There's an anxiety in the question, a question inconceivable 150 years ago when music of the day was the order of the day. Well, anyone who makes predictions is bound to be wrong, so don't look to me. Our main concern lies in the present. The present quality of contemporary classical music, at least in America, is actually pretty good. One might wish there were a larger public. Although perhaps the richest experiences are, by their very nature, unavailable to most people.

1999

Julian Green

Artists are always being questioned about their influences. They know the answer, of course, since nothing comes from nothing. But they hesitate. After all, they've made a career of covering their tracks: Indeed, the act of covering tracks is the very act of creation. What I shall now reveal, therefore, is something of an admission.

The news of Julian Green's death at ninety-eight reached me last July, just prior to a performance in Nantucket of a song by me on words by him. Fifty years earlier, when living in Morocco, I had read my first work of Green, a novel called *Moira,* and was stunned—like meeting my double in a trance. Narrated in compact Gallic language, the story treated an American disorder: sexual guilt of, and murder by, a horny inarticulate red-haired youth in a Southern university. New World puritan frustration via the mother tongue of Mallarmé. Green spoke American in French, the reverse of, say, Janet Flanner, who spoke French in American. We had an exchange of letters, and when I returned to Paris that fall we met. The meeting quickly veered toward a violent intimacy which lasted about ten months, during which I saw Paris through his eyes and the world through his pages.

Green's first novel, *Mont-Cinère,* came out in 1926 and changed the tone of French literature. The subject was family greed in our southern United States, the language was lean and somber. Similar juxtapositions occurred in this American's twenty-odd fictions over a period of sixty years, all but one composed in French. By 1951, when we met, he had also become, along with Gide, Europe's principal master of the diary, a format which, if no more "true" or "confessional" than novels or autobiography, is by its nature more immediate. So I took up my own diary again, influenced, in manner if not in matter, by his. By extension the influence must have touched my music too, though no one can explain quite how, at least not in words (for if the arts could express each other, we'd only need one art). In this same year was republished a brief memoir called *L'Autre sommeil.* Green was still in his twenties when it first appeared, but it speaks of his own death with a sadness that seemed . . . well . . . musical. I translated and made songs from three paragraphs. This is the music sung again last summer.

Green eventually wrote several modestly successful plays, one of which, *Sud,* was turned into an opera by Kenton Coe. In 1971 he was the first person of American parentage to be elected to the Académie française.

Julian Green was not a Thinker, much less a philosopher. If he had a riveting gift for plot, even in such an open-ended structure as the diary, the gift came as a stream of consciousness. "If I have anything to say," he wrote, "I'm hardly aware of it. If I do bring a message, then I'm like a messenger who is unable to read and whose message is incomprehensible to himself; or rather, like a stenographer who cannot read his work because he only knows how to write."

But he *was,* in a sense, a messenger. Like many a holy convert he was more Catholic than the pope, and his prose is permeated with a sort of hopeless hope that the world will be saved. Those perpetual obsessions with sin and the true way, with prayer and dream, with shop talk (Jesus talk) among clerical friends! If in his *Journal* Julian Green continues, through his specific belief in God, to miss more general points at every corner, in his fiction this very "miss" provides the Julianesque tonality, the singular Greenery. Surely if one-track-mindedness empties the spirit of humor, it does fill the mind with an explosive physicality which remains the *sine qua non* of all large souls. (Humor is not physical but rather intellectual, and multiple-track-minded.)

Such skepticism was apparent to Julian, who deplored my atheism, promiscuity, and what he termed "dangerous frequentations," and then there was the age difference of twenty-five years. He gave me his books, photographs, insight into a rarefied milieu, a plaster cast of Chopin's hand (which, to his horror, I used as a bookend), and, above all, confidences about his closeted yearning requited by his tactile love for a statue of Apollo. His stifled emotions, the very grist of his early novels, grew less repressed in the later years. "I don't care what anyone writes about me when I'm gone," he often said. And he often said too—quoting Pascal quoting God—"You wouldn't seek me if you hadn't already found me."

Which brings us back to influence. Is it cause or effect? Are we drawn to a work because of what we glimpse of ourselves already there, or do we discover only what we bring? Was my personal feeling—which was less than love and more than love—for Julian the man impelled by the unbearably wistful expertise of Julian the artist? Or was the unbearable wistfulness already in me, minus the expertise?

Today the expanse of time since first we met seems slight, yet surely I have at least a musical voice that has nothing to do with Julian Green. Though by another turn of the screw, I wouldn't be me if it weren't for him.

For the Academy   *13 April 1999*

For Judy, at the Players Club

Her initials are those of Joan Crawford, John Cheever, and Jesus Christ, combining glamour, intellect, and a high moral tone. Such is Judy Collins, who claims the added gift of instant likeability.

We had never met when, at a party for a mutual friend, I rang her bell. She opened the door, gave me a long look from out those violet eyes, then covered me with kisses. That was 100 seasons ago.

In the intervening years, the spontaneity has never stopped even when we're miles apart. Because, corny though it sounds, we continually share. I gave her the first taste of an anonymous but powerful group which has saved many a body and soul; also a wreath of songs which she sings from time to time. She gave me the sound of her voice made of—of what?—of unalloyed silver.

So I greet you tonight, dear Judy, with affection, admiration, and a waterfall of arpeggios. I love you. Ned

16 Gramercy Park   *2 April 2000*

On *Gore Vidal: A Biography*

By Fred Kaplan
Doubleday, 850 pages

World War II freed our music and painting. Isolated for a generation from crushing European influences our composers and visual
artists became identifiably American. As for literature, it already
had a home-grown tradition from Hawthorne to Faulkner; but the
prewar machine of Hemingway seemed suddenly shed by three
young southern WASPs, each unrepentantly gay in art as in life,
each valuable, but otherwise disparate. I knew them all. By 1947
Tennessee Williams, Truman Capote, and Gore Vidal—the latter pair a mere twenty-one—had become and remained celebri-
ties more famous even than their work: Williams our preeminent
dramatist, Capote the exemplar of well-tuned fey poignance, and
Vidal a solid novelist, polemical essayist, and sometime politico.
The trio was publicly perceived as colleaguel yet rivalrous intelligent adults given to childish feuds. It was an age of the writer
as star.

Of the three Vidal was the most level-headed, the most prolific, and had the most staying power. He has already outlived the
others' pathetic deaths by sixteen years, and is still going strong.
The strength is now commemorated by Fred Kaplan, biographer
also of Henry James, Dickens, and Carlyle. He opens with a lyrical

three-paragraph prelude describing the visit, with Gore Vidal
and Howard Austen, his partner of five decades, to the Washington cemetery where the two will purchase a burial plot. The plot
will lie equidistant between that of Henry Adams and that of an
obscure childhood friend, killed in the war, whom Gore much
later decided was the love of his life. This scene, related in the
present tense, is alive and delicious. The next eight hundred pages
are tough sledding, partly because much of the material is already
familiar from Gore's own autobiographical writings, and partly
because no detail is deemed slight enough to repeat (sometimes
several times) in Proustian-length paragraphs.

People's childhoods are much the same (wonderment, suffer-
ing) until the individual emerges. Only the settings vary. Gore's
setting was Washington government and the international society to which he had immediate access, and which would serve
as literary contexts for the rest of his life. His maternal grand-
father was an Oklahoma senator; his father an aviation specialist;
his mother a handsome cold-eyed alcoholic philistine who by a
second marriage became an Auchincloss, thus linking Gore to a
dynasty that included Jacqueline Bouvier Kennedy. His educa-
tion was high-class — St. Alban's, Exeter (where he shined as a
political orator) — with an extended stint in the army. He read
voraciously, and his early writing was influenced by Maugham,
that self-proclaimed first-rate second-rater. His artistic interests,
at least according to Kaplan, were books and movies; in the whole
biography is nary a word about painting, and scarcely more about
music. (Although Gore once told me it was he who suggested
Lord Byron as a libretto to Virgil Thomson, who then invited him
to collaborate on the opera.)

Gore's notorious aloofness, in work as in play, developed gradually; in adolescence "he was not really, at least publicly, egotistical" . . . "he was a dedicated non-liar who rarely lapsed" . . .
"telling the truth was a way of making the world more reliable."

His sex life was astoundingly active and is documented with vicarious relish by Kaplan, who never tires of telling us how gorgeous the young writer was, and how irresistible his physicality seemed even to such foes as Capote. He had "all the sex his expansive, virile desire could accommodate . . . sex but not love with strangers" picked up on the street or in steam baths. With few exceptions (the childhood crush on Jimmy Trimble, the dancer Harold Lang, Howard Austen with whom he still lives, but platonically) these non-sentimental male attachments numbered in the thousands over the next five decades. The women in his life — Claire Bloom, Anais Nin, Joanne Woodward — are depicted mainly as friends, if maybe one-sidedly in love with the writer.

During those same decades, and with the same vaguely objective urgency, appeared twenty-one novels, many of them best-sellers, and three of them — the equivocal *City and the Pillar,* the terrifying *Kalki,* the insolent *Myra Breckinridge* — groundbreaking sensations; two volumes of stories including the wryly original *A Thirsty Evil;* six collections of essays, arguably his most lasting work, and consisting of political tracts, book reviews (or Lit Crit, a term Vidal is proud to have coined), and reactions to stabs, notably a farsighted treatise on Midge Decter's homophobia. Add to this five plays and a bevy of film scripts (anecdotes about Charlton Heston's obtuseness to the gayish nuances of *Ben Hur* are hilarious), and you have an oeuvre of many million words.

Each of these works is carefully deconstructed by the biographer, as are the social and professional circumstances surrounding the initial impulse. Yet the analysis never comes alive. Of course, the pith of any art lies in the art itself, not in the critique. And perhaps Gore's style and language, as distinct from his substance and plot, are not memorable. His characters are all prone to talk alike, nor do we find the bigger-than-life "poetry" of Tennessee and Truman. Indeed, it would be fun to claim that Gore's Achilles' heel is in that above-the-fray position — he never bursts into tears. Yet

that very position defines him as man and artist. One cannot cen-
sure a stance per se, but only how well the stance is brought off.
Gore brings it off fine, and occasionally makes it into high art.

(Ravel, on his critics: "Does it not occur to these people that
I may be artificial by nature?" Gore himself wrote to his London
publisher, John Lehmann: "I agree . . . that one should not create
characters that are lifeless and dull merely because the originals
might appear that way; on the other hand I think creation of a
character in a novel is very much a business of chance; either the
magic happens or it doesn't.")

The most engaging moments are not in analyses of the work,
but in lengthy portraits of peripheral players. Read the intense
and canny description of the late 1960s TV dialogues with William
Buckley ("he had the ability to use language to simplify complex
issues and to complicate simple issues") and the ugly lawsuits that
ensued. Or the hot and cold rapports with Norman Mailer ("one
thing to be literary rivals, quite another to work actively to damage
him") whom Gore found to be a homophobe despite himself. Or
Angus Wilson on Gore ("flawed by intelligence"); or Jason Epstein
("[Gore] had too much ego to be a writer of fiction, because he
couldn't subordinate himself to other people"); or Gore on Truman Capote (whose death was "a good career move. T will now
be the most famous American writer of the last half of the twentieth century. No one will ever read a book of his again but no one
who can read will be able to avoid the thousands of books his life
will inspire"). Or even Ned Rorem ("Gore says, 'It's not that love's
a farce — it doesn't exist.' Defensible. Yet it's just one definition,
or something without definition. Rather than risk being called a
softy, he affects a pose of weariness. Still he remains in Italy. That
is a romantic decision as well as practical. Vulnerability is a major
factor in any artist's makeup. To disguise the fact is merely another
way of making art").

Now seventy-four, the "onnfont-tarribul" as Capote once called
him, lives mostly in Ravello where he and Austen entertain the

best minds and crowned heads of our globe. He fully cooperated, sight unseen, in this biography, which at half the length would be twice as good. As with all biographies the subject is only partly there. But Gore Vidal, nothing if not terse, might be more clearly depicted if his adulator followed suit. Meanwhile, Kaplan's book is an invaluable font of research on the subject, possibly the only one we'll ever need.

*1*999

Opening Remarks as President at the American Academy of Arts and Letters, 2000

What a pleasure to be standing in this hallowed hall for the first time as President, "to honor the old and reward the young." But which is which?

On learning of my appointment I sensed an irony: Presidents are grown-ups, so how did I qualify? And yet, while it's true that not all children are artists, all artists are children insofar as they perceive the open without the blinding pressures of survival. When the grown-up prevails, the artist expires. By that token, our stage today is one vast kindergarten—"the unacknowledged legislators of the world." Though Auden was quick to add: "Poetry makes nothing happen"?

Indeed, art does not change us—does not make us better persons. Art intensifies, makes us more of what we already are, shows us what we did not know we knew. Art is not real life but a concentration of life. When it succeeds as propaganda it can fail as art. Is it the inspiring music of a military band that impels soldiers into battle, or just the steady beat of the drum? (Though if I, as a Quaker, could compose a march to impel soldiers *away* from battle, I'd do so in a trice, and bid adieu to art.)

It is as a musician that I am a member of this century-old

institution. Now, the only professional as financially insecure as
the serious classical composer is the poet. How many of the famed
creators on this stage actually subsist from the just rewards of
their labor? Most poets earn more by talking about poetry than by
writing it. Composers get even shorter shrift. For the first time in
history the musical recreator takes precedence over the creator;
even the cultured public is more aware of the interpreter than
of what he interprets. Performers, of course, are not eligible for
membership in the Academy, the election to which is considered the highest form of artistic merit in this country. Still, in the
steady figure of 250 members, fewer than a fifth are musicians. It
was only half-facetiously that I proposed lengthening the title to
"American Academy of Arts, Letters, and Music," or shortening it
to the more comprehensive "American Academy of the Arts."

   In an increasingly money-mad and culture-foolish world, it
is oddly America, with its notorious vulgarity, which is the most
interesting and vital land of the new millennium. The admittedly
elitist stance of the Academy is that America's future, as in the
past, will be judged not by our economy or war power, but by
our lasting civilization as exemplified in writing, music, and pictures. Who can explicate such works? I can go only so far, even
with my own work. "The rest," as Henry James said, "is the madness of art."

At the Academy   *May 17, 2000*

American Song at the Millennium

Not one American singer today can break even exclusively as a recitalist, much less as a recitalist in his native tongue. If he manages to fill the hall, he does so on his reputation as an opera star, and the program is always studded with arias, watered down with piano accompaniment.

Forty years ago the Russian cellist Rostropovich commissioned a number of large-scale vehicles from composers all over the world. That he was also a great interpreter seems slight when you realize that, emerging from a creatively archaic country, he single-handedly caused to exist most of the important cello literature of that half-century. Imagine any American singer, emerging from this creatively advanced country, pursuing such a notion! None of them, not even for his immortality, has voluntarily paid for new works.

Europeans are general practitioners, and Americans are specialists in everything except recital song repertory. Young German or Italian or French singers master the problems of their native tongue first and foremost, and often spend distinguished careers singing solely in their own language. Young Americans learn every language except their own. Graduation recitals feature songs in German, Italian, and French, none of which the students "think" in; if they do offer an English encore it is tossed off with a fake foreign accent.

Due partly to the high majority of European teachers who deem English unsingable, partly to the opera-oriented bias of students themselves, the voice recital has atrophied in the United States. The students (those not aiming for musical comedy) sniff neither glory nor money in English-language repertory. They feel no pride in—have scarcely an awareness of—the long tradition of song in English. To declare as they do that English is ungrateful is to see clearly the thrilling pitfalls which in foreign languages are invisible. The only thing bad about English as a vocal medium is bad English. And the only thing bad about modern vocal settings is bad music.

If in the world of Elvis, song is a trillion-dollar business, in the world of serious classical music, song is the least remunerative of expressions. Song in English, particularly by Americans, is more rarefied still, partly because historically the form's intimacy never meshed with the massive concepts of our pioneer composers and partly because we have no recital legacy for singers. If you can count on the fingers of one hand the number of vocalists who subsist as recitalists, even they prosper more than composers. Today, re-creation takes priority over creation. The Three Tenors, intoning arias by dead Italians, earn more in one evening than what a live American composer earns in a lifetime.

Which is why so few American composers anymore specialize in songs. Singers won't sing them because there's no outlet, there's no outlet because there's no real money, there's no real money because managers are aiming higher, and the higher aim exemplifies the increasing philistinism of the concert world vying with international pop culture.

2000

Aaron's Songs

Aaron Copland, who with Hitchcock and Borges and a few marvelous others now fêtes his hundredth birthday, was the father of American music. American music, for the moment, will be defined as music penned by Americans between 1925 and 1955. We'll eschew the up-to-then German traditions admired by, say, Griffes and MacDowell, veering from the economical leanness promoted by Nadia Boulanger. Around 1955, the Serial Killers took hold with a featureless canvas that could in no way be defined as national. If Virgil Thomson was the first to borrow native Kentucky tunes and treat them symphonically until finally, like Poulenc in France, he composed his own folk music (so to speak—or so to sing), Copland improved on the practice, embellished it, taught it, and made it his own. *Appalachian Spring,* with its stress on spare harmony and homemade folksong, its dearth of counterpoint, its scoring without much doubling, and its fairly simple hand-clapping rhythms, defined American music for two generations.

Like all artists Aaron was a child, but where some play at being a grown-up, Aaron's childishness had a frank visibility that I've never seen elsewhere, except perhaps in Ravel, of all people. Someday I must expand a theory about their resemblance—in their target if not in their arrows. For although Ravel was lush where Copland was plain, both stressed the craft of *dépouillement,* of stripping bare. And has it ever occurred to you that in their "representa-tional" music they seldom portrayed the adult world? Ravel with his toys, his Daphnis, his affinity for animals, was *L'Enfant et les sortilèges* incarnate. Copland's Common Man was an abstracted man, like his ballet personages who were the eternal adolescents in the wide open spaces. He was forever drawn to the pubescent realm of *The Tender Land* and *The Second Hurricane*. Both men were urbane (they knew "everybody") but dwelt far from the mad-ding crowd, Copland in sophisticated innocence, Ravel in naïve sophistication.

But it is interesting too, since children's music is inevitably sung music, how few vocal works there are by Copland. Beyond the two brief operas just mentioned, what is there? Well, the first extant manuscript is a one-page fragment named "Lola," composed at age fourteen. And there were a couple of songs from the late twen-ties, and some little choral pieces from the films of the late thir-ties. Then in 1950, with the premiere of *Twelve Poems of Emily Dickinson*, a curtain was raised. Bliss was it then to be alive, at least for us young composers—all twelve of us—when every new work by Copland (or Stravinsky or Shostakovich or Britten) was greeted with ecstasy, and the land was still rich with the enthusi-asms of first-times.

Except for his arrangements of *Old American Songs* the fol-lowing year, this cycle was the first and last foray into the genre by Copland. If today Dickinson is the poet of choice for American song composers (you'd think there was no one else), the choice was relatively unhackneyed in 1950. The settings of the *Poems*, each dedicated to a fellow composer and each expertly self-contained, form a unified whole befitting cycles by Schumann or Fauré.

My favorite begins: "The world feels dusty when we stop to die/ We want the dew then, honors seem dry." I love Aaron too much to want to "honor" him. Instead, for this centennial, I offer him the preceding sentences like a dew-drenched valentine.

2000

Women and Minorities in Contemporary
American Classical Music

Asked to cite the twenty-one most interesting living American-born composers, I quickly name seven women, two black men, and twelve white men—half of them Jewish. They range in age from thirty-five to eighty-five, and six of them are gay.*

Women as performers have existed only for 250 years, mostly as vocalists. The noun "music" is feminine in all European languages, and though the art is sometimes termed effeminate, it has always been strictly a male domain. A soprano might demand and receive equal pay, because she's not replaceable by a man, but female flutists or drummers must fight it out.

Women as composers are of quite recent vintage. Unlike writing and drawing—crafts available to any child—musical composition supposes a lot of technical know-how, middle-men between maker and listener, plus rehearsals and the hobnobbing with

---

*The 21: John Corigliano, Richard Danielpour, David Del Tredici, David Diamond, Lucia Dlugoszewski, Deborah Dratell, Lukas Foss, Daron Hagen, Lou Harrison, Jennifer Higdon, Barbara Kolb, Ezra Laderman, George Perle, N.R., Christopher Rouse, Alvin Singleton, Michael Torke, Joan Tower, Melinda Wagner, George Walker, and Ellen Zwilich.

managers, conductors, and sometimes dozens of orchestra men all at once. This is not the usual accompaniment to housewifery. Our first women composers wrote salon repertory with titles like "Scarf Dance," gently accessible small forms dismissed as "ladies' music." Then, as more and more women turned professional, their music at first sounded so "masculine" that only a woman could have penned it. But if masculine meant loud and insistent, how account for the comparatively passive output of our presumably virile Faurés and Chopins, or of Griffes, and Theodore Cranler? Today, of course, an unalerted listener would never guess the sex, or even the nationality, of a composer. Feminist composers can no longer be identified as such in their non-vocal works, since music, unlike prose or pictures, has no concrete meaning.

Like women, our black population had no outlet for self-expression in creative music, except in the group participation of un-notated spirituals. Individuals, like William Grant Still, used programmatic titles like "Afro-American Symphony" and "Pages from Negro History," back in the teens and twenties. (I'm personally proud that my first piano teacher was Margaret Bonds, who left a legacy of arrangements of spirituals for both solo voice and orchestra.) Today black composers write music, not black music.

So do white male composers. As to the Jewish ones, they began to materialize about the same times as blacks and women. But today, unlike, say, Bloch or Milhaud, or even Leonard Bernstein, they do not compose what could in any way be called Jewish music.

Two women, Ellen Zwilich and Melinda Wagner, have finally won Pulitzer prizes, as has the African-American George Walker.

Who are the male WASPs that I elect? Well, I'd include two trentenarians, Michael Torke and Daron Hagen, and two octogenarians, David Diamond and Lou Harrison. Beyond them, I daren't name names for fear of being stoned by those I've omitted.

As for the six gay ones, outing is not my business. Let's say only that what was until recently named Gay Sensibility is just a slogan masquerading as an idea. When people ask me if there is a gay sensibility, I answer: Define it; then I'll tell you if there is one. I, however, am gay, and I also got a Pulitzer, back in 1976, when such wicked ways were looked on askance.

Now, with all the evolution, where do we composers stand? Since there are no longer stigmas against blacks and Jews and gays and women, we're one big happy family. (Our music is the music of ourselves, not our groups. Not gay, or black, or Jewish, or female, or WASP music. Just music.)

So the only stigma might be said to be against composers as a whole. In fact, to the managerial establishment as to the overall public, a black gay woman is no more discriminated against than a straight white man. Composers today are not so much tolerated as just invisible.

2000

On Learning of Paul Bowles's Death

Deaths which are "not unexpected" because they come to the very old are sometimes for that very reason the least expected. Thus, for us among his friends who knew he'd been ailing for years, the eighty-eight-year-old Paul Bowles's demise in Tangier seemed nevertheless impossible; for if he could die, so could we all. And thus, on hearing the news yesterday morning, I felt madly wistful—a feeling one might not expect for this man who was seemingly so removed from demonstrable reaction.

Still more contradictory was Phillip Ramey's report on the phone. The body will be shipped to France for cremation (an illegal practice in Moslem countries), the ashes returned to Morocco, then brought to America next February. They will then be taken by Phillip and the photographer Chérie Nutting to upstate New York, and buried with the Bowles parents and grandparents. These were Paul's wishes. For one who hated the United States, who loved the Sahara, and whose wife, the underrated novelist Jane Bowles, lies in a Spanish cemetery, one might have expected a site less sentimentally homey.

If all artists are the sum of their contradictions, then Paul Bowles is an extreme example of that definition. Throughout his nearly nine decades he practiced two parallel careers which seemingly never overlapped.

In 1949, with the publication of his very successful *Sheltering Sky* at the age of forty, Paul Bowles became the author-who-also-writes-music, after having long been the composer-who-also-writes-words. That success brought more than a reemphasis of reputation; from the musical community's standpoint it signaled the permanent divorce of a pair of professions. During the next two decades Paul Bowles produced fourteen books of various kinds, but little more than an hour's worth of music. Did he feel that one art, to survive, needed to swallow and forget the other? Surely he received in a year more acclaim for his novel than he had received in a lifetime for his music. This need not imply a superior literary talent; indeed, if history recalls him, it may be for his musical gifts. It's just that ten times more people read books than go to concerts.

Composer-authors generally compartmentalize their two vocations, allotting parts of each year, if not each day, to each career. But as authors their subject is invariably music (witness Berlioz, Schumann, Debussy, or Boulez, Sessions, Thomson), whereas Paul Bowles was a fiction-writing composer, the only significant one since Richard Wagner, and even Wagner's fiction was at the service of his operas. Except during the war years when he functioned as a music critic, Bowles's prose was antithetical to his music. Whatever resemblance exists between the working procedures for each craft, the difference between his results is like night and day.

His music is nostalgic and witty, evoking the times and places of its conception—Paris, New York, and Morocco during the twenties, thirties, and forties—through languorous triple meters, hot jazz, and Arabic sonorities. Like most nostalgic and witty music that works, Bowles's is all in short forms, vocal settings or instrumental suites. Even his two operas on Lorca texts are really garlands of songs tied together by spoken words. In 1936, Orson Welles's production of *Horse Eats Hat* became the first of some two dozen plays for which Bowles provided the most distinguished incidental scores of that period. The theater accounts for a huge percentage of his music output, and for the milieu he frequented for a quarter-century, most latterly the milieu of Tennessee Williams whose works (*The Glass Menagerie, Summer and Smoke, The Sweet Bird of Youth*) would never have had quite the same tonality—the same fragrance—without Bowles's melodies emerging from them so pleasingly. Indeed, the intent of his music in all forms is to please and to please through light colors and gentle textures and amusing rhythms, novel for the time, and quite lean, like their author.

Paul Bowles's fiction is dark and cruel, clearly meant to horrify in an impersonal sort of way. It often bizarrely details the humiliation and downfall of quite ordinary people, as though their very banality were deserving of punishment. Bowles develops such themes at length and with a far surer hand than in, say, his sonata structures. His formats in even the short stories are on a grander plan than in his music; at their weakest they persuasively elaborate their plots (albeit around ciphers, and in a style sometimes willfully cheap); at their best they transport the reader through brand-new dimensions to nightmare geographies. Bowles communicates the incommunicable. But even at their most humane his tales steer clear of the "human," the romantic, while his music can be downright chummy. Indeed, so dissimilar are his two talents that it is hard to imagine him composing backgrounds to his own dramas.

Paul Bowles's real life was courageous and exotic. Whenever possible he spent it in what we like to call backward countries with hot climates, especially Ceylon and North Africa, like Prokosch before him, and Maugham. Yet no matter how far afield he wandered, he maintained active correspondence with the West, specifically American intellectuals who, since he seldom went to them, crossed oceans to meet him. Bowles, the social animal, traveled Everywhere, knew Everyone, and was much loved (though he never admitted to loving). His writings dealt extensively with the Everywhere, but never with the Everyone, until the auto-biography, *Without Stopping,* which failed.

We met during the summer of 1941 in Mexico, where I was traveling with my father who felt I should get away from the cor-roding arty homophilia of our native Chicago. How little did he know! Paul was thirty, I sixteen, good-looking and with a roving eye. Paul later would pen a story, "Pages from Cold Point," about an adolescent in Taxco who seduces many a local male including his own parent. Naughty gossips suggested that . . .

———

Paul, meanwhile, was the first professional composer I'd ever encountered. He introduced me to the music of Copland and Thomson and, especially, himself. The main soprano aria from his zarzuela, *The Wind Remains,* with its recurring drop of a minor third—the so-called Mahlerian "dying fall"—so bewitched me, that to this day it has been the single most telling influence in my several hundred hours of music.

For the next sixty years we saw each other fairly regularly, over there and over here, and otherwise we corresponded. The corre-spondence, *Dear Paul, Dear Ned,* was published a few years back, by Elysium Press, with an introduction by Gavin Lambert.

How can I say how lucky I feel that this document remains of the most confusingly interesting, distantly lovable, gifted and reti-cent man who ever lived? The world weighs less with his departure.

Read at the YMHA   *30 October 2000*

A Few Words on Ned O'Gorman's
New and Selected Poems

We share the same Manhattan zip code. I used to wonder if the area were large enough to contain two such Neds. But we complement each other. He is outward and rugged, if not too self-revealing; I'm effete and neurotic and a bit self-pitying. And I'm transparent, while he's dense — and sometimes hard to understand.

Yet is art ever understood, rather than felt? Can music be proved to mean anything? Can poetry (any poetry, from Mother Goose to T. S. Eliot) be scanned so as to have the same literal significance for all readers? Art, like love — or hate — is intuited rather than parsed. And since opposites attract, I'm drawn to Ned O'Gorman, even as he says he is to me.

One can experience his verse as one experiences the loss of virginity, or the finding of a hundred dollar bill on a park bench. He tells us what we did not know we knew. Look, for example, at the novel but unforced rhymes and images in "Winter":

> The matter of intellect is arctic.
> . . . and the reign
> of intellect collapses on petrified oceans of snow.

Or the carnality of "Vegetable-Life":

> Where the pulp lifts its germ and the sludge
> of beauty lies.

Or the fright—yes, the fright—in "A Rectification of the Lyric":

> There is
> nothing left at all, anywhere.
> Place has ceased to be . . .
> . . . time is broken in the corner
> of the eye.

Or his take on love in "A Philosophy":

> . . . Love is not easy and likely to trouble dreams.
> . . . It is man's way of life . . .
> until the end of love; until the body's end.

Or his unwitting reuniting of old acquaintances in "Fulco di Verdura: A Vanity." I knew and liked Fulco a half-century ago, and lost him, then found him again in Ned's poem. Likewise I found my alcoholism of yore in "Drunk on the Lord's Wine," but now it's turned to faith.

"Peace, After Long Madness," echoing Yeats's rhythms, as "Panther" echoes Cavafy's, is a boon to any insomniac. "Ram" is sheer sex, and so in a way is "Dreams Erotic, Dreams Not." I could go on for pages.

For I deeply need Ned's poetry. Like his name, it is part of my life.

2001

On Charles Ives

On the occasion of Chen Yi receiving the Ives Living Award

First, let me thank everyone for coming to share in Chen Yi's thrilling honor. Thanks also to Louis Auchincloss's hospitality, and as always to Virginia Dajani for her unflagging help offstage and on.

Since brevity is next to godliness, in society as in art, I'll keep these words on Charles Ives down to five minutes.

There is a wonderful irony in this occasion: Who would have thought, when Harmony Ives bequeathed the estate of her comparatively unknown husband to the Academy fifty years ago, that the Ives Living Award, inaugurated in 1998, would become the single largest prize ever created for composers? Except for Copland, Ives is the most-played American in the world today. His royalties have made it possible for the Academy to give—to date—168 scholarships, 22 fellowships, and now the Ives Living; yet he himself never felt comfortable accepting money for composing. He printed much of his work at his own expense. His younger colleague, Henry Cowell, editor of New Music Edition, a nonprofit company whose slogan was, "If it will sell, we don't want it," claimed Ives once told him that when a big commercial publisher planned to publish his violin sonata, he didn't know what to do because he didn't want to accept money for his music.

I first heard Ives's name when I was nineteen. A colleague and mentor, Lou Harrison, was giving me a crash course on the ways of the avant-garde. There are only three composers, said Lou: Ruggles, Varèse, and Ives. He was at that moment re-orchestrating Ives's Third Symphony, of which he would conduct the world premiere in 1946, thirty years after its composition. Lou also played for me the Ives orchestral *In the Night,* which, in its weird blurred sadness, changed my life. Remember, said Lou, Ives is a "primitive," like Satie. But of course in music there are no "primitives," a certain minimum of know-how is needed to notate. And Ives was as complex as Satie was simple. So complex, indeed, that his music hardly ever was programmed. Like William Carlos Williams in New Jersey earning his living as a doctor, Ives made a fortune in Connecticut with his insurance company.

He was born in 1874, one year before Ravel, and died in 1954, three years after Strauss. But he stopped composing in 1926. During the 1930s, when a bit of acclaim came his way, mainly as an utter original and an utter American (because he composed pieces for three town bands playing simultaneously using hymn tunes, and because, like Cowell and Harry Partch a generation later, he used a quarter-tone scale)—at this time, according to Lou, he would pre-date his new publications to make them seem more path-finding, and sometimes add a few "wrong notes," as Prokofiev also did, for the same reason, or as the French novelist Jean Genet did by embellishing the cruelty of his adolescent incarcerations. But isn't any device a creator employs valid, if the end result convinces?

Ives's end result convinces. In the year of the composer's death, Balanchine created the extraordinary ballet *Ivesiana,* using the now-famous *The Unanswered Question.* The title is derived from Emerson's poem "The Sphinx" and later was used for Leonard Bernstein's Harvard lectures. Balanchine also choreographed *Central Park in the Dark,* wherein the sixty members of his company, thirty stage left, thirty stage right, all on their knees, crawl toward, and then *through,* each other, and disappear as the music fades.

That Ives never heard, or saw, or read, these versions of his art, is both poignant and somehow relevant. Poignant, because music, unlike the other arts, needs to be interpreted in order to exist; relevant, because if Ives had physically been more in the stream of things, he wouldn't have been Ives.

As to how Ives may have reacted to the present occasion, I'll let the committee chairman, Ezra Laderman, take the chair, as he introduces our guest of great honor, Chen Yi.

2 Feb. 01

re: Visible Man

Eminem's music may well be "great art," as Mim Udovitch suggests, but this can't be learned from Udovitch's essay. Not one sentence is devoted to the music per se, as distinct from the text which has been set to the music. When the noun "music" is used, what Udovitch means is the lyrics, or, more generally, the song.

Song, conjoining the crafts of tune and verse, is more than the sum of its parts. In all song, from Beethoven to the Beatles, it is the melody which lends force to the lyrics. Classically, most songs were devised on pre-existing poems (sometimes centuries old), while popularly the lyrics are by the composer himself. But the words are what lend "sense" to the tune. Pure music, i.e., non-vocal music, unlike poetry or painting, cannot be proved to have any meaning at all; it is the text, not the music, which represents the intellectual power, or indeed the danger, of any song. No strict symphonist, unlike a Goya or a Mapplethorpe, can be charged with subversion, much less with being rebellious or revolutionary.

Until we learn that the word "music," as used by most pop critics today, is actually a metaphor for text, their analyses fail.

Letter to the New York Times   19 *Feb. 01*

re: Defining Opera

A year or so ago Stephen Sondheim and I had a lively public argument at the Y about what Opera is. "The sole definition is that which happens in an opera house," claimed Sondheim; *Sweeney Todd* thus becomes an opera when performed at New York City Opera. Now Bernard Holland adopts that definition as final in his essay on Sondheim. Couldn't one then ask: Do *Dido* and *Tosca* and *Grimes* become showbiz musicals when heard in a Broadway theater?

May I suggest that the difference between Musical Comedy (or Tragedy) and Opera is not aesthetic but practical, not a matter of art-versus-entertainment but of the kind of voice a composer had in mind. Madonna could never perform *Manon* any more than Callas could belt pop. True, an Eileen Farrell is occasionally cited as a "convincing" jazz singer, but the inverse convinces no one—witness Streisand's trammeled pretensions in *Classical Barbra*. It's not that pop singers haven't the scope of op singers (though they haven't), or that op singers can't fake a bluesy whine while continuing to roll their Rs. It's that the *need,* and hence the literature, of each genre is disparate. This need dominates the earliest training of each kind of vocalist. Thus composers are faced with separate constructional considerations for each genre.

The genres, like church and state, have run parallel forever.

Whatever the musical speech or philosophical sense of a lyric theater piece, that piece's definition rests on the composer's technical intent: It may be termed Opera only if composed for operatic voices, and Musical Comedy only if composed for musical comedy voices. Why not term the two genres Variable and Invariable? Insofar as "Lonely Town" or "Send in the Clowns" or even "Summertime" are plausible sung by any sex in any key with any arrangement, they are variable, and so the context from which they spring is not Opera. Insofar as *"Un bel di"* or *"Voici ce qu'il écrit à son frère Pelléas"* or even "Pigeons on the Grass" are not plausible except as sung by the sex and voice they were conceived for, in one key and orchestration, they are invariable (set arias, if you will), and so the context from which they spring is opera.

Only in America could this argument rage. If our cultural inferiority complex, still at this late date, is saved by hiring European conductors for our leading symphonies, the same inferiority asks us to dignify a recent and unique commodity — musical comedy — with the name Opera, as though opera with its long and tacky history were a serious sign of worth.

E-mail to the Arts & Leisure Section, New York Times   *July 2001*

For Robert Starer

Because we led parallel lives our paths seldom crossed. We went to different schools together, so to speak; and even when we were both at Juilliard, we majored under different teachers. But if "to know well" means acquaintance-with-the-essential rather than mere frequentation, we were intimates. His every new work was admired by me, and somewhat wistfully envied, as when his four ballets for Martha Graham outnumbered my own. In some ways we were alike, being, along with Paul Bowles, the only American composers who were also professional authors on matters other than music. But our histories were deeply distant.

Born in Vienna in 1924, Robert Starer entered the State Academy of Music at thirteen. One year later, with Hitler's annexation of Austria, Robert was routed from the school—to the sneers of certain classmates—and fled with his Jewish family to Jerusalem. He continued his studies at the Palestine Conservatoire, served with the British Royal Air Force during the war, and after it came to New York for post-graduate work, first at Juilliard, then with Copland at Tanglewood. In 1957 he finally became a U.S. citizen, and thirty years later was named a Distinguished Professor by the City University of New York. Among his honors are two Guggenheim Fellowships and grants from the National Endowment and the Ford Foundation. In 1994 he was elected a member of this

Academy, received an Honorary Doctorate from the State University of New York, and a Presidential Citation from the National Federation of Music Clubs. He also was granted a Medal of Honor for Science and Art from the President of Austria, the very country he was forced to flee a half-century earlier.

Robert was quadrilingual. Indeed, the only words he ever wrote to me were on a letterhead in Hebrew, Arabic, English, and German. His music by turns was a sumptuous mix of Viennese Expressionism, chromatic dissonance, with more than a trace of Arabic and Jewish folk tunes, plus raw American jazz. And all of his oeuvre was highly theatrical; not just the violent ballets, and the four operas (two with librettos by his partner, Gail Godwin), but the String Quartets, the Guitar Preludes, the smallest songs.

Consider again the 1962 *Phaedra,* wherein the leading dancer, contemplating her suicide, just sits. And sits. And sits. Robert was able to depict motionless silence through musical sound.

Or listen again to the three String Quartets. The Bartokian virility of the First is translated somehow into Hebrew. The melancholy Andante from the Second seems gorgeously undefinable, while the tender mysteries of the Third (composed just five years ago) become a balm in our rough times, forcing the corny comment that We Happy Few outlive our bodies.

Now listen to the opulent innocence of the Ravel-ish String Duo; and to the diatonic French-ish settings of the choral psalms and Talmudic stories, surreptitiously braided with augmented seconds and other near-Eastern accents. Indeed, when I hear Starer's music I hear again his own spoken accent, so very faint, and see again his reddish hair and serious face. Are these evoked too in the early Clarinet Quintet, with its lean, heartbreaking, Coplandesque nostalgia and literal incorporation of Catskill folksongs, so far from the hills of Israel?

All this talk, of course, is mere description, a critic's business, and none too vivid. But even if the medium of words could describe the medium of sound, the essential would still be lost. I've listed a few of Robert's influences because, as Rimbaud claimed, art is "clever theft." Aware of his crime, the artist attempts a disguise; the act of disguising is the act of creation, and that act is the gift of our greatest geniuses. Lesser artists may be more "original," but not so ingenious. Still lesser ones, unaware of their theft, are merely derivative. If one can locate the origins of most of Robert's ideas, one cannot describe how these origins become *him*; for individuality, as distinct from influence, is finally undescribable.

Robert Starer also penned three books: an early school text, a memoir called *Continuo,* and a novel called *The Music Teacher.* These may not outlive the music, but they are skilled in their own right. And, like his enviable piano-playing, are preserved in publication, representing the backgrounds I've named.

Robert said: "Other features of the cultures I have known did not become part of me. This has led me to believe that while our lives are shaped by events that others control, we do have the choice of accepting from the worlds around us only what can co-exist with our essential self."

At the Academy   *8 Nov. 01*

For Morris Golde's Memorial

Sometimes I tell people that I've been married nine times, but never divorced. If that's the case, my first spouse was Morris Golde. After one passionate year our love-that-was-more-than-mere-friendship evolved into a friendship-that-was-more-than-mere-love and remained so for six decades.

It began in 1943, when I was attending Curtis in Philadelphia, far from my native Chicago. I used to come up to New York every few weeks to hear concerts and cruise bars. In one of the latter— the Old Colony on 8th Street—toward 3 on a July morning—I met Morris, and we lurched back to his place on the top floor of where he lived until the end, at 123 West 11th. Like most nineteen-year-olds I was wildly sophisticated and wildly naïve. I was drawn to Morris's tough Bronx accent, which belied his vast culture. Working by day at the Michael Press, which he founded with his brother, and where the young Barbra Streisand was at the switchboard, by night he read Kafka (whom I'd never heard of) and listened to Beethoven, whose quartets I'd only just come to know. Indeed, with all that butch swagger, he was the most culti-vated man I knew, his closest friends including the tenor William Horne, harpsichordist Ralph Kirkpatrick, and pianist Hortense Monath, who founded the New Friends of Music.

The unique angle of Morris's love for art and artists was that, not being an artist himself, his magnanimity bore no trace of competitive envy. His press printed free brochures for his professional friends. He was generous with time and—perhaps more important—with money. And for me he was helpful in strictly practical ways with my problems as a young composer. He had answers. If it weren't for him, I wouldn't be me.

Lauren Flanigan and I will perform two songs of mine which somehow seem apt for Morris Golde's memory. "What If Some Little Pain," words of Spenser, was composed in 1949, and concerns death as a welcome release from life. "Early in the Morning," on a poem of Robert Hillyer, was composed in 1954.

13 November 01

The Intelligence Quotient

We learn from television that Mozart can raise your child's I.Q. Then we see shots of kids jumping rope, accompanied by the G-minor Symphony.

The concept is insulting both to Mozart and to the children. The children are not listening to the music; they are merely hearing it as a steady beat to keep the game going. Since music, good and bad, has long been used as wallpaper—for parties, in elevators, at the A&P—it has become simply background. In the case of Mozart, it's not the form and texture but the regular rhythm that makes the point. The rhythm could as well be that of Ravel or the Rolling Stones.

Music has nothing to do with intelligence, or even with culture—or how do you account for so many educated intellectuals, including major creative writers and painters like Kafka and Picasso, being tone-deaf? Nor does music improve us so much as make us more of what we already are—or how do you account for Nero fiddling while Rome burns, or Nazis playing Beethoven quartets to drown the prisoners' screams? Music is not morality, and many a miraculous musician, starting with Wagner, is no better than he should be. To use music as therapy is to belittle the composer.

Certain sociologists making this study allow that, yes, Mozart does raise a child's I.Q., but only for ten minutes. Can they tell us what lucid revelations arose and vanished during this wondrous period? Does it mean that their own adult I.Q. was briefly raised?

I'm a bit weary of Mozart forever being invoked as the one genius about whom we all agree; and that if we could concoct a computer for churning out masterpieces, the computer would be based on Mozart's brain. Now, if I proclaim that Mozart is not an Absolute—that, indeed, he is not a genius—can you prove me wrong? Greatness is a matter of opinion, and until we all have one opinion we will never be able to concoct that computer to indoctrinate our children. But then, in that perfect world, our children wouldn't need indoctrination.

Suppose we did successfully clone Mozart. This creature, emerging into the twentieth century, might not care for music, might not like "Mozart" but only rock 'n' roll, and might contain only the many banal qualities of his model.

2001

For John Corigliano
at the National Arts Club

In thinking over what I'd say tonight, it struck me that composers, after a certain age, don't hang out much together. When they do, they talk less of deep meaning than of commission fees. The rest is silence of creation, or advice to students.

John Corigliano is for me an exception to this rule. We've been meeting regularly—that is, maybe once a year—since 1965 when he visited me about his programming at WBAI. He was twenty-three. We were drawn to each other because, in a time dominated by Serial Killers, we both wrote from the heart (though my heart was colder). The ensuing four decades for each of us have produced a mass of vocal settings, in his case a wreath from Dylan to Dylan. (Dylan Thomas, that is, and Bob Dylan.) But *The Ghosts of Versailles*, after its Met premiere in 1991, had the same sociological effect as Menotti's operas two generations earlier. If Menotti and Corigliano could make it, in this least American and most costly medium, so could we all (went the reasoning). Today everyone's composing operas again—all because of John.

He also has works of every instrumental size and shape. Unlike most musicians today who come to their trade by hook or by crook, John was raised in the heat of the fray: His mother was a gifted pianist, his father the New York Philharmonic's concertmaster since before John was born. I remember years ago going with John to a bank vault from where he drew forth his father's Stradivarius, swathed in green velvet, and caressed it, just to make sure it was still there. Which surely accounts for his emotional expertise in the soundtrack of *The Red Violin*.

John has changed the face of our music while remaining fairly conservative. It is not a new language he speaks, but a new pronunciation of an old language.

The last time I came to this room was to assist at a similar honor for Judy Collins, to whom I said, "Your initials are those of Jean Cocteau, Joan Crawford, John Cheever, and Jesus Christ, combining originality, glamour, intellect, and a high moral tone." To these initials let me add those of John Corigliano, who enjoys the above virtues with an added dose of his own wizardry, wisdom, and wit.

21 March 02

Opening Remarks as President
at the Academy, 2002

Welcome to the 104th annual ceremonial of the American Academy of Arts and Letters whose purpose is to honor artistic achievement with awards amounting to nearly a million dollars.

If a plane crashed into this hall today international culture would be forever damaged. When a moth drowns in Africa, a sycamore in Oregon trembles, however faintly. No living thing is an island; all life is interconnected. The events of September 11th confirmed this definitively. Many an artist on that day wondered, what difference now do my so-called creative acts make? A week later he knew; they make every difference. For our civilization will be judged in the future, as it has always been judged in the past, by its arts and not by its armies — by construction more than by destruction. The art, no matter its theme or language, by definition reflects the time. A waltz in an hour of tragedy, a dirge during prosperity may come into focus only a century later. Is Picasso's *Guernica* any more trenchant than Jane Austen's *Emma* or Debussy's sonic portrait of an ocean?

This is the third and last time I will address this assembly as President. The first time I mused on how this dignified status seemed a fluke: Wasn't I too young for such a job? Then I reasoned that all artists are children and if they grow up they stop being artists, so I was as qualified as the next one. The second time I announced that brevity is next to godliness so let me be sanctified for only one act as President: that of shrinking this lengthy ceremony by twenty minutes, in dispensing with the reading of credentials of those honorees not present. I also suggested (in vain) that our title be shortened to merely the American Academy of the Arts, or stretched, to the more correct American Academy of Art, Letters, and Music.

Today, as already hinted, I feel more downbeat. True, if this hall were destroyed now, we'd still have the works of the dead, but those works seem increasingly distant to the living public. True again: Art does not uplift us, nor make us better persons; art makes us more of what we already are by telling us what we did not know we knew. But if the arts have grown remote, it is especially the art of music about which I am most aware. Even to some otherwise well-rounded intellectuals in this very Academy, simplistic Rock has, for whatever reason, come to represent *the* music of today, on a par with the world's best painters and authors.

Ours is the only musical era in history where the past takes precedence over the present, where the performer takes precedence over the composer. A successful violinist earns in one evening what most composers in this room earn in a year, and he earns this by playing almost solely Mozart and Beethoven. Yet this situation is invisible in the light of the quadrillion-dollar industry of Rock. There are fewer than a hundred American critics of classical music; most of our best periodicals have completely dispensed with such criticism, and the dumbing-down now officially includes the *New York Times* and National Public Radio.

World population swells annually, but the number of our cognoscenti seems to remain stationary. So does the 250 membership of our American Academy. Even without a plane crash the high-quality artistic segment within a mediocre but prosperous world appears fading. Which is why, as I wave farewell, I at least feel good about the admittedly elitist stance of an Academy which, though minuscule in representation, is massive in scope.

At the Academy   *May 16, 2002*

Henry Cowell

In our pedophilia-obsessed day, it is interesting to recall that Henry Cowell, in 1936, received a heavy sentence for having fellated a seventeen-year-old boy. Had Cowell paid off the boy's family he might have been spared four years at San Quentin. Although he claimed it was too noisy there to write original music, and that anyway his scores were thought by his jailers to be "codes," he did organize an inmates' band, and also completed one of his most ravishing pieces, the *United Quartet*. In 1940, thanks largely to efforts of Sidney Robertson (whom in 1941 he married), Cowell was released from his fourteen-year sentence, into the custody of Percy Grainger, to be his "musical secretary."

Not all of Cowell's friends were sympathetic. Charles Ives (1874–1954), now America's most widely known experimental musician, never quite "forgave" his younger colleague. Cowell meanwhile promoted Ives's work as avidly as Mendelssohn promoted Bach a century earlier, placing him forever on the international map—another proof, if proof were needed, that great artists aren't necessarily great human beings, while many saints are second-rate artists.

I met Henry Cowell twice, both times at Virgil Thomson's in the early sixties when the three of us, plus Vladimir Ussachevsky, were (unsuccessfully) plotting to revive New Music Edition. In the glare of Virgil's rapid wit Cowell struck me as self-effacing if willful, without much glamour. Had he been dulled by the prison term? by his selfless efforts to support others? by encroaching disease? I never saw him again. He died in 1965.

———

John Cage has a name our world knows; yet he might be unknown were it not for the now-unknown Henry Cowell. Indeed, Cowell's pupils, Cage and Lou Harrison, Gershwin and Burt Bacharach, have tended to outlive him, like so many of his more flamboyant colleagues (Ruggles, Partch, Varèse, Seeger, Antheil, Schillinger), partly because of his publicizing them. Now comes a book, *Essential Cowell*, to reinforce that notion. In forty-eight prose pieces he discusses the music of almost everyone but himself — and of himself there is no value judgment, only technical explication.

Kyle Gann's preface in itself is a perfect review. If he opens by declaring that "Henry Cowell was the one composer who seems to have come out of nowhere," then contradicts this with "Charles Ives used tone clusters years before Cowell," one is merely reminded of Radiguet: "A true artist cannot not be original; he has therefore only to copy to prove his originality." Gann briefly outlines Cowell's work and life, which began in 1897, stressing the man's "utter refusal to be hemmed in by, or overly impressed with, the past. . . . Like John Cage, Cowell could say, 'I can't understand why people are frightened by new ideas. I'm frightened of the old ones.'"

But it is the late Dick Higgins, poet and actor, who has sewn together selections from Cowell's huge catalog of prose, some of it mere wisps, some in-depth essays, all of it didactic and with little style but much content. The best of the writings (1921–1964) are from the thirties, and are as much analyses as appreciations, i.e. the words on Stravinsky, and on Virgil Thomson wherein he extols simplicity as radical.

The seven sections are divided thus:

"HC in Person" relates a trip to Moscow in 1931 with its attendant trials of communication, and the unexpected things that
happen at concerts, partly due to unusual political situations. But
Cowell believes that "it is largely because of the vital part that
music plays in the lives of Russians. We here are apt to regard
music as a mere amusement. To the Russian music is a deeply
ingrained necessity for the outpouring of his feelings." Higgins
notes that Cowell's expressed abhorrence of communism is a
reflection of McCarthyite hysteria still in the air when he penned
"Music Is My Weapon" in 1954. I myself resist Cowell's state-
ments like "I believe in music: its spirituality, its ecstatic nobility
. . . its power to penetrate the basic fineness of every human being."
(Like, for instance, the Nazis who played Beethoven quartets to
drown out the screams of their victims?) Or: "Unexpected inner
response to the power of music dedicated to human integrity that
might reach dictators more easily than an atom bomb." This, from
a man who was tortured for four years at San Quentin.

Part Two discusses eighteen contemporaries, from Ives through
Sessions to Bartók. Here we find rare traces of humor, as in his
thorough discussion of musicologist Nicholas Slonimsky. "If you
wish to be in a position to converse freely . . . at cocktail parties
about sisquitone, quadritone, quinquetone, and diatessaron scale
progressions, or to engage in profound discussion of, let us say,
the sesquiquinquetone progression of an equal division of eleven
octaves into twelve parts, Slonimsky's *Thesaurus* is an absolute
must for your library." Meanwhile, the chapter on my beloved Lou
Harrison is less on Lou in particular than on percussion in general.
("The full possibilities of percussion . . . have hardly been tapped
in our symphonic literature.") As I grow older I use less and less
percussion and feel almost morally against all drums; if I never
hear another cymbal crash it won't be too soon. Percussion is inevitably used as reinforcement, for emphasis; non-pitched percussion is seldom integral, but decorative, like too much lipstick.

Part Three: "Music of the World's Peoples" is marvelously

researched, and related by one who's been there. Likewise Part Four, where Cowell dissects three of his own works. Part Five, in 1934, tells us of collaborations, and conclusions, with dancers, from Hanya Holm to Martha Graham. Years later, in 1967 when Graham choreographed a work of mine, I could only concur with Cowell that she won, hands down, not by dancing to the sway, but by going against the music; she made me hear myself as I never had before.

Part Four, "Musical Craft," discusses the process of so-called creation, the nature of melody, and the Joys of Noise, presenting the view that pure noise would be the basis of the next music after the liberation of dissonance. ". . . a loud sound does not touch our emotional depths if it does not rise to a dynamic climax." What about Satie? Or Debussy's piano *Préludes*? The margins of my copy are littered with approving asides or cranky wrist-slappings. "How true!" I jot to "Meaning is imparted to melodies, very often through inflections similar to those in speech"; but "Isn't it the reverse?" I ask, to "speech is given meaning by its tonal inflections. Melody, in music, rests fundamentally on the same sorts of inflections." In *The Process of Musical Creation* of 1926, Cowell answers many a lay question. "The most perfect instrument in the world is the composer's mind." "I rarely change a note after a composition is written." But ". . . only about ten percent of the musical idea can be realized even at the best performance," forces me to reply, "Maybe closer to ninety percent." Et cetera.

Henry Cowell's own music, stripped of percussion and other "effects" (wordless sliding voices, plucked piano strings, etc.), is far from forbidding. Listen, for example, to the swooningly contagious final Largo from *Four Combinations* (1921): It offers no problem, beyond the one of dealing with sheer beauty. If the theatrical suite *Atlantis,* four years later, is a series of *trouvailles* for human voices, those *trouvailles* are less formally integral than an overlay of tricks (squeaks, grunts, wails) erupting around and above quite diatonic music. The sum impression is madly spooky, but impressive it remains, not a new language like, say, Schoenberg's, or even Harry Partch's.

Music was Cowell's whole life. If, with his wife Sidney, he covered ninety thousand pages with words *about* music, he produced a hundred thousand with music *toute courte,* including twenty symphonies. It is for the latter that he will doubtless be judged by the future. For the present, I'm inclined, with Wallace Stevens, to stress "Not ideas about the thing/but the thing itself."

July 2002

For Lou Harrison

In 1944, age twenty, I earned my living as Virgil Thomson's copyist. I labored daily at his dining room table, while he ran the world of music over the telephone in the nearby study.

One morning out of the blue there sat another person at my worktable. Tall and big-boned but somehow fragile, like Orson Welles on a tulip stem, effusive but stylish, obsessed with how music looked on the page, this was Lou Harrison. A California composer six years my senior, he had worked with Schoenberg and with Henry Cowell, with whom he had founded New Music Edition for publishing what was then deemed experimental work. Now he was uprooted for the first time, about to begin a stint as a stringer for the *Tribune*, and meanwhile helping Virgil with extra copy work. More skilled than I (Lou's hand-drawn musical and prose artifacts are world famous), with a practical sense of performance broader than mine (he had formed his own percussion orchestra with John Cage), and with a grasp of intercultural workings that surely exceeded my grasp, Lou became Virgil's valuable colleague. Indeed, Virgil might have let me slide out of sight were it not for his devotion to my cause; nor was Lou interested in replacing me. As it was, we got along famously: Lou as a person was a total original, as a composer a total eclectic. His social style was Californian, easy-going, even Oriental, but with more than a tinge of daftness which led later to a turn in the loony bin (his term), and with a predilection for Negro males.

His music style was anything that was asked for; Lou felt that one ought to be capable of all, and had earned a living from choreographers (twenty-five dollars a minute was his fee) of every persuasion, composing fandangos for José Limón, folkish diatonicisms for Jean Erdman, Webernian mood pieces for Charles Weidman. Lou taught me the whole bag of tricks of the so-called twelve-tone system in about an hour, and I applied them for about a week. Finally, however, his eclecticism was original. Lou Harrison sixty years ago was concocting raga-type ostinatos identical to those today of Glass or Reich, with the notable difference that while all three men prepare canvases that are nonpareil, only Harrison superimposes a drawing—a melody—upon the canvas, which gives it a reason for being.

Weekends we would gather at Lou's on Bleecker Street, where he lived with his black clergyman, and while swilling quart after quart of Schaefer beer, talk of his idols, Ives, Ruggles, and Varèse, artists he pitted against Copland, whom he disdained. Lou adopted me, was helpful in many ways, for he had his foot in every door. It was he (I *think* it was he) who gave me entrée to certain organizations that performed me, like the International Society for Contemporary Music.

Lou Harrison was born in Portland, Oregon, in 1917. In San Francisco during the war, along with the percussion concerts with John Cage, he worked as a florist, records clerk, poet, dancer and dance critic, playwright, and nurse in an animal hospital. He invented the "tack piano," an upright keyboard with thumb tacks in the hammers to create a metallic sound. Moving east in 1943, he wrote for *View, Modern Music,* and the *Herald Tribune.* He conducted

too, giving in 1946 the first complete performance of Ives's Third
Symphony. The next year he received a grant from our Academy,
then left to teach at Black Mountain. In 1952 and '54 he received
Guggenheim Fellowships, and in the latter year visited Rome,
where Leontyne Price premiered his opera, *Rapunzel,* which won
a 20th-Century Masterpiece Award. There followed in '55 a commission from Louisville for *Four Strict Songs* to his own Espe-
ranto texts on some of his continuing concerns: love, plant growth,
peace, and concerted enjoyment on the journey to death. His
involvement with pacifism and his concern for freedom are evident in later works, notably the puppet opera *Young Caesar,* on an
early homosexual affair of Julius Caesar, probably the only "gay"
opera hitherto composed, with the possible exception of Britten's
Death in Venice.

During the late 1960s Lou Harrison, on a Rockefeller Grant,
went to live in Korea. His lifelong obsession with pitch relations,
in particular just-intonation, and his interest in music of other
cultures, led him to include non-Western or folk instruments in
dozens of his works, and eventually inventing his own, including
jade flutes, wash tubs, and muted iron pipes. But since his intrin-
sic language is melodic, diatonic, and very simple, I, for one, prefer the works that depend less on what seem like frantic sound
effects and more on sheer tune. For instance, the haunting 1950
Suite for Cello and Harp. He had just completed a work called
Nek Chand for a Hawaiian slack guitar and corrected final proofs
of a book of poems plus some gamelan scores and drawings, when
he dropped dead last February at a Denny's restaurant in Lafay-
ette, Indiana. He was eighty-five.

———

There is no right time to die. A child's death is really no more
tragic than an old person's. As for our own death, Freud claimed
it is unimaginable, "and when we try to imagine it we perceive

that we really survive as spectators. . . . In the unconscious every one of us is convinced of his own immortality."

But for artists, immortality is a given. Thus Lou Harrison will continue living, not just in the minds of us brief mortals who knew him, but forever in our recordings and concert halls.

13 November 2003

Foreword to *A Pocketful of Music*

For Martha Braden

Ours is the only era in history wherein the musical past dominates the present. Ninety-nine percent of serious concerts feature the three Bs, avoiding most French repertory and anything contemporary. Up until around 1915, performer and composer were the same man (Beethoven, Chopin, Liszt, Rachmaninoff) playing his own music. With the advent of impresarios the two separated. The interpreter became the star. Today a successful pianist or cellist earns in one evening what a living composer earns in a year, and he earns this by playing long-dead creators.

Now realize that the above paragraph pertains only to what we term "classical music." This music, even in the ken of the educated public, is mostly ignored, replaced by pop and rock. I and my brothers and sisters are not even a despised minority, for to be despised you have to exist, and we are invisible. Such dumbing-down infects our earliest learning. If yesterday high school courses included Music Appreciation, today—since there's no money in it—"high culture" has gone the way of the dodo.

But along comes Martha Braden's valuable anthology. Like Schumann's *Kinderscenen* or Debussy's *Children's Corner* or indeed Bach's *Inventions*, the anthology may be easily heard by the very young but played only by the adult pianist. Martha will expand elsewhere about the aim, which is "to aid those parents and teachers who wish to raise a new generation of listeners, persons who see the arts as essential to the spirit of the larger community."

I pray that it is not too late for active participation in an art that in another generation could be lost forever.

November 2003

On Becoming a
Chevalier dans l'Ordre des Arts et des Lettres

This award means more to me than any others, because it is the most personal.

In 1949 I sailed to France for the summer. But instead of the summer I remained eight years. To the question, "Did all that time in France influence you and your music?" the answer is: I went to France because I was already French, not the other way around. It is not the going home (though we may never have been "home" before) that makes homebodies of us; we are homebodies, so we go home.

If the universe is torn between two aesthetics, German vs. French, extravagance vs. economy, superficial depth vs. deep superficiality, warm vs. cool, then I fall roundly into the second category. Maybe because I was raised a Quaker, I was always drawn to the restrained Catholicism of the French, their music's immediate sensuality, their writing's witty melancholy, their painting's precise impressionism.

Si ce n'était pas pour la France, je ne serais pas moi. Je lui dois tout.

Merci.

At the French Consulate in New York   *12 January 04*

re: *Dylan's Vision of Sin*

As one who has always found Dylan-the-singer charmless and rasping, Dylan-the-poet sophomoric and obvious, and Dylan-the-composer banal and unmemorable, my feeling was not changed by Jonathan Lethem's review of Christopher Ricks's book. Lethem's complicity with the author, in equating Dylan with Blake and Picasso, no less, must embarrass even Dylan.

Yet assuming he is right (though what is "right" in such matters?), Lethem has not one word to say about the music; when he says "music" it's a synonym for lyrics. Since ancient times songs sink or swim on the quality of the music to which the poems are set; but Lethem has no opinion, much less an analysis, of *how* the tune and harmony and instrumentation relate to the text.

As for the giggly postscript by Lucinda Williams, she does refer to Dylan's "sweet beautiful melodies," as well as to his influential "sweet-ass attitudes," but such notions are meaningless in responsible criticism.

Letter to the Editor, New York Times Book Review   *June 13, 2004*

"With More Than Love"

How long does love last? people ask, meaning the Romantic Love of passion and heartbreak. Answer: three years. Of the classical Great Loves—Romeo & Juliet, Pelléas & Mélisande, Tristan & Isolde (the love potion they inadvertently shared was meant to wear off after three years)—the protagonists all die young. One can't imagine them as middle-aged folks putting their kids through school.

Yet all love is eternal, for love exists outside of time, and is obsessive and selfish. The French call it *l'égoïsme à deux*. One person over the decade can declare "I will love you forever" to thirty different people and mean it every time.

My own literary concern with love began in adolescence when I read the modern classics of Europe: Gide's *Counterfeiters* and Mann's *Death in Venice,* both about an unrequited older man and a boy; Pierre Louÿs's *Aphrodite,* about an Alexandrian courtesan; Cocteau's *Les Enfants terribles* about a brother and sister. I memorized these books and, in a way, relived them.

My longest "affair" was with Jim Holmes. We lived together for thirty-three years until his death in 1999. The physical lust faded after the first thirty-six months. Then our rapport bloomed into shared concerns—musical, political, educational—which were surely broader than "mere" friendship. Indeed, we signed our occasional notes to each other: "With more than love."

For the Valentine's Day issue of the
Washington Post Book World   *2005*

For Phyllis Curtin

Improvisation, in speech as in music, is foreign to my nature. So allow me to read these scattered notes in the five minutes allotted.

From one viewpoint Phyllis is the most important soprano in the world. The viewpoint—or earpoint—is, of course, my own; but by extension it is that of all modern composers, especially composers of song. That the living composer is central to all music should also be—but alas! no longer is—the viewpoint of the listening public.

Ours is the only era in history wherein the performer is more apparent than what he performs, and what he performs is always music of the past. Our composers are not even a despised minority, for to be despised you have to exist, and contemporary music is invisible, even to most intellectuals. As for singers, they are on a lower rung than instrumentalists. Opera stars, of course, are famous, and the women are as crucial as the men, since they cannot be replaced by men. But singers of song are a breed apart, especially in America where recitalists sing in every language but their own; and when they do sing in English they roll their Rs.

The difference between opera and song is the difference between prose and poetry. Both are theatrical, of course, in that both are artificial and invariable; but it's the theatricality of

overstatement vs. understatement. In song, clean diction goes far-
ther than histrionics. An example: In 1957 a long fast song of mine
was premiered by the electric Patricia Neway. The words, by Elizabeth Bishop, concerned a visit to a mental hospital. Since I was
at the keyboard I couldn't see Neway, but did hear her swoop and
yell, and did perceive some quick motions with her hands around
her head. At the end she got a standing ovation, her hair falling
to her shoulders. She had been removing hairpins, like a mad-
woman. This was a performance from inside-out. Next evening
in another part of town I accompanied Phyllis Curtin in the same
piece. Phyllis performed from outside-in. She described rather
than declaimed; and since the diction was flawless her underplay-
ing was more chilling than Neway's performance.

Recently Phyllis phoned for the first time in a year. "I just
wanted to say—don't you *love* Song!" Now that she's retired from
the stage her life still revolves around singing. If she is frankly jealous of younger singers, and wistful too, she *has* become America's
most effective teacher of singing—no, not singing, but of Song.
All her life has been Song. Her daughter, Claudia Madeleine,
was named for the Italian soprano Claudia Muzio, and for Madeleine Milhaud, still thriving in France at 103. My file of Curtin memorabilia contains an equal amount from her husband,
Eugene Cook, who, as a professional photographer, immortal-
ized her long career.

That career contains a huge repertory of opera roles, for the
Met and for international companies: from Verdi and Strauss and
Wagner to Britten and Walton and especially Carlisle Floyd. As a
concert artist she sang often with living Americans, notably with
Aaron Copland and with myself. In 1970 two of these recitals were
broadcast; three decades later they were issued on a CD for which
I wrote the following program note:

"Has it really been thirty years since we gave this recital? Soon
it will be forty years, then a hundred. The melancholy wonder of
recording is that the past becomes the present. The dead walk

again, though never with the same gait. For life changes meaning even as it's being lived, and the generations finally are irretrievable. Music itself, even to its composer, shifts its own significance with each passing day.

"I first heard Phyllis—Phyllis *Smith*—in 1946. She was one of the nieces in Tanglewood's production of *Peter Grimes*. At twenty-two I was ripe for her unusual (even more unusual today) admixture of nectarine sound with a sharp-as-ice diction. To say that Phyllis is the most *intelligent* soprano I've ever known is not to denigrate her, despite that adjective's frequent function to disguise other lacks. Throughout her career her delicious voice has never been used for its own sake but rather as a medium to impart the sense and feel of a text. For her—rare creature—the composer comes first.

"Not for another twelve years did we actually work together. Then for two decades we joined regularly in concerts sacred and profane. If our program, half me and half 'them,' had the interest of a living composer as pianist (common parlance before our century, then forgotten until the 1940s when Poulenc and Bernac revived the practice), still the presumption that the composer is an authority on his own music is, yes, presumption. I like to think that I learned as much about performance from Phyllis as she from me. If what I composed came first, she, as interpreter, literally had the last word."

10 May 05

For Edward Field and
The Man Who Would Marry Susan Sontag

To: Andrew Sawyer, the University of Wisconsin Press
re: The Man Who Would Marry Susan Sontag
by Edward Field

In style unmannered yet personal, and in form part-memoir/part-essay, Edward Field revives the dead. These dead—a gay literati both female and male—who might otherwise remain forgotten, now breathe again through his unique perspective. The hearts of composer Ben Weber, of writer Alfred Chester, of poet Frank O'Hara, throb vitally once more. Field also reanimates an era: of deranged psychoanalysis, of genteel anti-Semitism and pro-communism, of the artists' colony Yaddo when it was far more formal, and of the rapport between painters and performers. I have never had a more vitalizing experience. Since I personally knew the bulk of his cast, reading Edward Field is like awakening into his dream.

30 May 05

re: New Overtures

Instead of using "dinner and dancing" and other unrelated lures for the dwindling public of classical music, why not use more relevant programming? The last eighty years have been the sole period in history wherein music of the past takes precedence over the present. Today any work of a live composer is balanced against a hundred works by Mozart or Beethoven (or Brahms or Dvořák), whereas in *their* day, *their* music was the rule. This is not true of our American literature (indeed, the current *Times Book Review* is entirely devoted to contemporary authors), or the visual arts (living painters command huge prices), or the theater where a play by Ibsen—or even Tennessee Williams—is called a "revival." But we do not speak of a "Beethoven revival" where Beethoven is the rule. And I cannot think of more than one or two living composers of serious classical music who support themselves *as* composers rather than as teachers or performers.

I won't retract a word of my essay written forty years ago, which began: "I never go to classical concerts anymore, and I don't know anyone who does. It's hard still to care whether some virtuoso tonight will perform the *Moonlight* Sonata a bit better or a bit worse than another virtuoso performed it last night."

Letter to the Editor, Arts & Leisure Section,
New York Times   *21 August 05*

On David Diamond

Many laymen hold the notion that so-called Creative Artists, even famous ones, are all suicidal alcoholic misfits. But for every Rimbaud or Mussorgsky or Pollock, each of whom died young, there are scores of sober artists who are not especially colorful as personalities; their color is saved for their work. Might one argue that artists are the best adjusted of citizens? They know what they want to do, are able to do it, and are appreciated for doing it, without wasting time on eccentricities. Yet one may also argue that they are the only humans that resist generalities.

For example David Diamond. While being a prolific first-rate composer, he was in many social ways a mess.

He had the saddest eyes I've ever seen. I saw them first in 1944, when I was twenty and David thirty. He was sitting with his friend the painter Allela Cornell while she sketched dollar-portraits of passersby in Washington Square. I had long heard about him: his morbidity, his profuse gifts, his unapologetic homosexuality, his public obstreperousness. Now here he was, looking as if the world were at an end. A few months later Allela killed herself, leaving to David an apartment above a garage on Hudson Street. There he lived for the next seven years, until the Serial Killers took over our musical world, whereupon he moved to Italy.

During this period I was close to David in a master-pupil

arrangement. I worked as his copyist in exchange for lessons in composition and orchestration. I did score-&-parts of the Third and Fourth Symphonies, the Second String Quartet, and sundry smaller works, mostly songs. As his copyist in those pre-computer days I was accountable, after the fact, for each note in relation to itself and to the thousands of surrounding notes. As his student I was accountable, before the fact, for each sequence of notes that I would pen. David's years with Nadia Boulanger had shown him acute communication through both words and music. To this day I recall his every syllable: He taught me to write *perfect* music. (As to whether that music could breathe and bleed is beyond anyone's control.) He was my deepest influence then, both socially and musically.

David dazzled us all with talk of his dear friends like André Gide and Lana Turner, Maurice Ravel and Greta Garbo. If fact and fantasy were confounded, the result was nonetheless intriguing.

Like his friends, the texts for his 200-odd songs were diverse, ranging from the Bible and Shakespeare through Shelley and Joyce, to cummings and—yes—Marilyn Monroe. These songs were immediate: They "spoke," were diatonic, prosodically immaculate, and were featured on every American singer's program back in the days when American singers deigned to perform in their native tongue. His non-vocal music, including ten String Quartets and eleven Symphonies, was highly formal, eighteenth-century in structure, contrapuntal, even fugal. And though he composed no performed operas, he wrote a great deal for the dance, especially Martha Graham; for six movies, when Hollywood used real composers; and for the theater, where, nightly for a year, he conducted his own lavish score to *The Tempest*. Otherwise he earned a living teaching, and as a violinist in Broadway orchestras.

He was world-famous before turning twenty, a favorite of Koussevitzky, Dimitri Mitropoulos, Munch, and Bernstein. After the eclipse in the 1950s, he experienced a resurgence on returning from Europe. He taught for some time at Juilliard, then retired to his native Rochester, where he died last June, four weeks short of his ninetieth birthday.

If David was his own worst enemy (assaulting conductors at rehearsals, getting assaulted by sailors at midnight), he was also gentle and compassionate. In 1945 he was responsible for the publication of my very first songs. Forty-three years later, when my parents died, he sent me these words: ". . . I can write about death and dying but find it difficult to talk about. Your words, 'so now they're both gone,' tell me so much of what you have passed through. But what extraordinary human beings they were! I truly feel I respected them more than anyone else, more than my own parents, more than Dimitri. . . ."

By this time the wild life was behind him, as it was behind all of us who survived. The reasoning went: Anyone can dissipate, but only we can write our tunes. And David Diamond's greatest work lay just before him.

He was a swell cook too, even with his strong death wish. Already at nineteen he wrote a song to a John Clare text that begins:

> The world is not my home, I'm only passing through.
> My treasures and my hopes are all beyond the sky . . .

Yet his greatest treasure—the vast catalogue of expert music—remains here on earth forever.

At the Academy   *Nov. 10, 2005*

On the Modern Listener

A unique contradiction seems embedded in the typical American classical music lover of our century: He likes only what is far in time but close in space. Shunning the music of today, he nonetheless favors old music from his immediate culture. Contemporary American music is as foreign to him as the classics of China, while the classics of Western Europe soothe him more than any nineteenth-century composer from the East.

True, music is not a universal language but an attitude, of one consciousness and of one environment, that does not easily slip past the customs inspector. We are not all the same—it is difference, not increasing similarity, which lends Earth's dwellers their beauty, wisdom, mystery, and indeed, their identity. But if this identity is never fully grasped by a dweller from another environment, sometimes it can be sensed, appreciated, and even loved, especially if the identity lies in works of art.

Along these lines, might I suggest some music which contradicts the contradiction. It is from near in time, but far in space. A garland of Armenian song, from bass-baritone Ara Berberian and pianist Sahan Arzruni, that could satisfy the needs of any fancier of Schubert *Lied*. The arch and ebb of the tunes, although conceived mostly by recent composers, reflect a folkish prosody that borrows, as *Lied* does, from surrounding cultures—Greek, Turkish,

Arab, Russian—while retaining its signature as Armenian. That local signature lies in the ictuses of the native tongue, just as American music—even non-vocal music—can be distinguished from British by dint of mirroring the emphases of its composer's spoken language. My meaning will be clear the moment you hear the virile velvet of Berberian's bass-baritone as it rises and falls (with what passionate intelligence!) to the inspiration of his countrymen, and the caringly expert pianism of Sahan Arzruni as it limns the sad, old, gay, and above all, flowing melodies to which he was born. I myself was born a midwestern WASP and weaned on Ives and Griffes. But when I heard these Armenian songs, I felt they too were mine.

2005

My Music and Politics

Like all so-called creative artists—indeed, like all humans with brains—I am a net of contradictions. Born and raised a Quaker, I still adhere to the philosophical tenets of that group, yet I am an atheist. I do not believe in God, yet some of my most inspired music has been settings of scripture from both the Old and New Testaments. For I do believe in Belief, and in the beauty of works that have, in the name of God, come to be. It is, in fact, with a certain poignance and a vague envy that I observe true believers at work and play, for I know I shall die without faith.

I believe in the value of all life. I am a pacifist, a term I find beautiful (as did my mother and father), yet a term derided by some conservatives. Those same conservatives have nonetheless embraced me in their press, perhaps thinking that because my music is conservative (in the sense that it retains the values of yesterday), I am in all ways on their side.

I do not believe that music can be political (not, at least, in the sense that it can change us), can make us believe something we have not heretofore believed. Music has nothing to do with nobility or goodness, nor with evil or vanity. Music does not alter us; it confirms.

Music reflects; political speeches alter. Military marches supposedly help us march into war, but in fact that's not music but hypnotism—the regularity of the beat. If, however, I could pen a piece that would make us march *away* from war, I would do it in a trice, at the expense of my whole career.

Insofar as music does change us, it's not very good music.

2005

What Does Music Mean?

I've been living with music all my life and still don't know the answer to this question. Surely music's the most immediately persuasive of the seven arts—can any of the others make us weep, or fall in love, or recall the past? Yet *how* does music do this? Is the ear more sensitive than the eye? Or is it that our whole body is affected, as when we are moved to dance?

But if music can be proved to have concrete meaning, it's only music with *words*, not the notes, which is the proof. For words are symbols of specifics like "tree" or "rain" or "Tuesday," or even "and" or "but." Chords and phrases are possibly symbols too, but of what? Music cannot depict "yellow" or "spoon" or "Jennifer," much less "perhaps" or "if." If a composer writes a non-vocal tone-poem with a programmatic title, we envision the action, but only after having read the program. The music means only what the composer tells us, *in words,* it means. Play *The Pines of Rome* for an unalerted listener and tell him it's *The Fountains of Rome,* and he'll be none the wiser. Play *La Mer* for the same listener, and say it depicts three times of day, not at sea, but in Paris: Les Halles in the morning, a slaughterhouse at noon, and a dance hall in the evening. Again, he'll be none the wiser.

True, certain vast generalities seem recognizable through music: Love, for example, or Death, or Weather. Yet, the concept of Love as expressed through swooning strings stems from Wagner; before him the convention was more sedate, as with Monteverdi, then Schubert; after Wagner the convention turned coarser, as with Shostakovich's naughty trumpets in *Lady Macbeth of the Mtsensk District* or Ravel's scorching *Boléro*. As for Death, the minor mode did not signify sadness even two centuries ago (witness "God Rest Ye Merry, Gentlemen"), while the major mode in ancient Sparta was banished for its lasciviousness. Only Weather seems inarguably representable in music, and that's through onomatopoeia: A gong stroke *is* thunder, high piano tinkles *are* raindrops.

In music's so-called abstraction lies its power, especially when combined with theater. A slow score can bog down a scene at the racetrack. Fast music might make a courthouse scene seem silly. Music can weaken a strong script, strengthen a weak script. . . . Years ago, a piece of mine called *Eleven Studies for Eleven Players* was choreographed by several companies. It was fun for me, if not especially revealing, to watch lithe bodies doing the obvious — leaping to the lively sections, writhing to the mournful sections. Only when Martha Graham put her hand to the same music did I realize the potential, indeed the need, for the juxtaposition of mediums. In one movement, where the music goes mad with breakneck brasses blasting, she had a male dancer simply stand silent, moving his head ever so slightly. In another movement, where the slow tempo scarcely budges, she had a female dancer gyrate hysterically. Martha's imagination lent a whole new sense to my score, and by extension to her choreography, simply by going against the music.

To state that all music is abstract, all painting representative, and all literature concrete, is to state the obvious. Sure, they can be joined, as in song and dance, and thus shift their sense, to some extent. But they are not mutually inclusive. After all, if the arts could express each other, we wouldn't need more than one.

2005

George Rochberg

The melancholy of these readings is always relieved by a certain elation. For, alone among us, an artist does not die when he dies. His work can last for centuries, and that work contains what is unique to him, and is communicable and healthy, though he may socially have been bad or a bore. George Rochberg was neither bad nor a bore, but he certainly remains alive — even to those who never knew him — through the heartbeat of his music.

Non-vocal music, unlike all the fellow arts, cannot be proved to have even general meaning, like Death or Weather or Love, much less specific meaning, like Bread, or Tuesday, or Pencil. Mendelssohn said, "It's not that music is too vague for words, it's too precise for words." Usually I skip a composer's program notes, since his music speaks louder than words. But Rochberg contradicts at every turn my glib French generalities. He once wrote: "Making the world a better place is not a project for the artist. His project is to express the fire in the mind, to make, as Browning said, beautiful things that 'have lain burningly on the Divine Mind.'" (Of course art — at least visual art — expresses ugly violence as well, like *Guernica* or Goya.)

Another of my generalities is on music that falls into categories: the Melodic, like Chopin and Rachmaninoff; the contrapuntal, like Hindemith and Palestrina; the rhythmic, like Varèse or Bartók; and the Harmonic, like Debussy or Thomson. But Rochberg blends these simultaneously into a fifth category, which could be named Color. Listen to his Second Symphony of 1955, which opens like Beethoven's Fifth, becomes unstoppably loud and fast, then dissolves into a gorgeous minute that seems apologetically wistful. Or the *Imago Mundi* of 1973, an utterly tonal borrowing of the traditional Japanese school of printing—or in his words: "... a picturing of the external world—but only insofar as our pictures are imaginings, mental fictions, shadowed reflections of the 'reality' of past as well as of present times." Or the Violin Concerto of 1974, which opens like Prokofiev, and where again the fast parts are chromatic and frantic while the slow parts are diatonic and the color of tears.

His borrowings are kin to the creative process, since nothing comes from nothing. If you know you're stealing, you try to cover up your traces, and this covering is you. For example, his two-clarinet riff is right out of *Petrouchka,* which Stravinsky in turn swiped from *Rapsodie espagnole,* which Ravel had taken from Spanish folk song.

George Rochberg was born in New Jersey eighty-seven years ago. He studied composition at Mannes School until 1942, then served in the infantry in Europe until the end of the war. The war, said he, "was more than an interruption in my musical life. ... [It] shaped my psyche. ... I came to grips with my own time. I came to the necessity of the twelve-tone method independent of the few other American composers who turned to it after the war." Gravely wounded in France, he returned to Philadelphia. During the 1950s he worked at Curtis and at the University of Pennsylvania, then moved to Italy on a Fulbright and the Rome Prize, befriending Dallapiccola, leader of the Italian serialist avant-garde. Back in America, he published much prose on what he considered musical truths, and broadened his creative idiom to include tonal trends. He was performed around the globe.

Then in 1961 his son died at the age of twenty. Much has been made of Rochberg's ensuing despair, his struggle to give sense to serialism which now seemed shallow and arbitrary. He used his son Paul's—as well as his wife Gene's—texts in his work. Bit by bit he found a new language that was neither aleatoric nor serial, dialects that now seemed ornamental to a basic tonality.

Up through the 1980s, he was awarded our major honors, and grew as famous as a composer can be, before he died in the light—or is it the shadow?—of appreciation.

———

With the perspective of hindsight one finds that those long-gone "modern" composers who changed languages many times—Stravinsky and Copland, for instance—actually retained their same accent. Similarly Rochberg, at least to my ears, spoke the same language throughout his long life, despite what occurred away from his desk. For an artist at work stops living in order to write about living; should he weep real tears, they would smear the ink.

Yes, his music was always tuneful, if not in a conventional sense, nor harmonically lush. And it was always scary, at least to my ears, in both counterpoint and rhythm, as witness the ominous and persistent kettledrum slitherings in *Black Sounds,* or the original monodrama *Phaedra,* on Robert Lowell's verse which the human voice speaks and screams. Pure theater.

Indeed, all art is Theater, in that art is not real life but a concentration of life. By that definition the art of George Rochberg is Theater to the core, a core that is eerie, explosive, complex, and very sad.

At the Academy   *6 April 06*

PART III

Composer's Program Notes

(1974–2006)

Air Music: Ten Variations for Orchestra

Air Music could have been subtitled "Chamber Music for Orchestra," since much of it is for intimate groups, yet groups obtainable only when a symphony is at hand. The overall tone is of understatement, an immense miniature. Form, however, and not color, is the unifying force, and so I subtitled the piece "Ten Variations." The term "variations" is used as dancers use it: The variations are on each other rather than on an initial statement, for there is no theme proper. The movements share traits (shapes, hues, rhythms, tunes), but their resemblance is more that of cousins than of siblings.

1. Full orchestra (seventeen vertical blocks)
2. Full orchestra (nine canons with interludes)
3. Winds, strings, and solo piano (a two-part invention)
4. Tuba and violin solos, flutes and oboes, and all violins and contrabasses
5. Three clarinets, three trumpets, snare drum, and pizzicato strings
6. Cello solo with higher strings, plus one trombone and piano
7. Three flutes and three groups of violins
8. Viola and bassoon solos, four horns, and harp

9. Three oboes and three groups of violins
10. Full orchestra (a two-part invention with interludes)

Why *Air Music*? Because I'd already composed a *Water Music*, as well as a *Day Music* and a *Night Music*. And because, when the piece was finished, I came upon this apt quote from Wilhelm Heinse (1749–1803), which stands as an epigraph: "Music touches the nerves in a particular manner and results in a singular playfulness, a quite special communication that cannot be described in words. Music represents the inner feeling in the exterior air. . . ."

1974

———

Air Music won the 1976 Pulitzer Prize.

Violin Concerto

In the movie *A Woman's Face*, when Joan Crawford is asked what music she likes, she replies simply, "Some symphonies, all concertos." Why is the concerto so universally attractive, not just to dilettantes, but to amateurs and connoisseurs as well as to professional performers of every age? Because the concerto is the least abstract of the non-vocal forms while retaining, as the case demands, the highest seriousness. No matter how dense the language, any listener can hear—can *see*—what's going on. What's going on is a struggle, sometimes vicious, more often amorous, always necessarily harmonious, between the one and the many, and the one (with whom we identify) is a sympathetic technician.

But what *is* a concerto? Is it, as textbooks tell us, a three-movement sonata for soloist with orchestra? Then what of Falla's Harpsichord Concerto, whose "orchestra" contains but five players? Or Bach's Italian Concerto, with no orchestra at all? Or Bartók's Concerto for Orchestra, which asks for no soloist? Even virtuosity is not always a cause, as with Handel and Haydn, and some concertos have many more (others less) than three movements. Well, a concerto is a concerto if the composer chooses to call it that, and even he may switch his definition from piece to piece.

The present work is my seventh in the genre. (An eighth, for

organ, will exist by the time these words are read.) The first, a
three-movement Concerto da Camera for harpsichord and seven
instruments, dates from 1946 and has never been heard. A one-
movement Piano Concerto, written two years later, was quickly
consigned to a trunk, where it shall ever repose. Piano Concerto
No. 2, in the required three movements with cadenzas, was composed in 1950 for Julius Katchen, who premiered it beautifully
in 1954. Yet another such work for piano, called Concerto in Six
Movements, was commissioned in 1969 by Jerome Lowenthal,
who played it many times and recorded it. Meanwhile, in 1966,
Water Music, a small-scale double-concerto for solo clarinet and
violin, flowed forth. And another double-concerto, for cello and
piano, named *Remembering Tommy,* comes from 1979 and is cast
in ten movements.

The Violin Concerto, begun here in Nantucket five weeks ago,
was completed this morning, August 25, 1984. It could as sen-
sibly be called Concertino since it is small-scale, or Variations
since each movement depends thematically on the others, or Suite
since the six titled sections imply a narrative. Certainly it is not
conceived in so-called sonata form (except insofar as that form is
actually the slickest version of Theme & Variations); indeed, it's
been ages since I've tried, in the academic sense, to "develop"
my material. I conceive all non-sung pieces as though they were
songs—like settings of words that aren't there. And I stop, or try
to, when my idea is used up.

Twilight is formed from a rambling prologue followed by a slow
melody for strings, over which the soloist sews a countertune like
lace on velvet. *Toccata-Chaconne,* built on a twenty-three-times-
repeated figuration in the timpani, rises jaggedly from a purr to
a thunderclap, then reverses itself and fades back into a purr.
Romance Without Words, the title borrowed from Mendelssohn,
is literally a song from which the text has been excised. (In 1953
I set Paul Goodman's "Boy with a Baseball Glove" for voice and
piano. Now, thirty-one years later, I remove the verses, nudge the

tune infinitesimally so that it suits the solo violin, orchestrate the accompaniment, and offer it here.) *Midnight,* a microcosmic variation, is itself a Theme & Variations. *Toccata-Rondo* is in spirit a false waltz, that is, a waltz in 4/4. *Dawn* recalls *Twilight,* one tone lower, with the solo and orchestral roles exchanged. (The tune, incidentally, derives from incidental music composed for a play called *Dusk,* again by Paul Goodman, decades ago.) As to the story, if there is one, unfolded through the six sections, let the sounds divulge it.

Not until I'd finished did I realize that the solo part contains no "effects" and no cadenza—just a few harmonics scattered like stars into *Midnight.* As for the orchestra, why is it so sparse, with only five woodwinds, a trumpet, timpani (in but two of the movements), and strings? Because I had just finished *An American Oratorio,* which calls for everything including the kitchen sink, and I felt the need to dispense with extra color—and even with necessities, like the sink.

Since program notes should be as economical as art, let me add only that the singular virtues of violinist Jaime Laredo were constantly with me as I worked: the electric verve of his style, the gentle strength of his intellect, and the unrippable silk of his oceanic tone.

Postscript: Another movie, *Humoresque,* also contains a classic line. When Miss Crawford learns that her violinist protégé doesn't like martinis, she understands. "They're an acquired taste," she explains, "like Ravel." (We shall expand on this in the next lesson.)

1984

The Auden Poems for Voice, Violin, Cello, and Piano

---

1. The Shield of Achilles
2. Lady, weeping at the crossroads
3. Epitaph on a Tyrant
4. Lay your sleeping head, my love
5. But I Can't
6. Yes, we are going to suffer, now; the sky
7. Nocturne (Make this night loveable)

Composers compose. If they had trouble weaving their musical ideas, or even finding musical ideas to weave, they wouldn't be composers. Trouble, at least in the case of song composers, lies in finding apt texts to clothe with their notes. The most arduous process in confecting a cycle, as distinct from a miscellany of songs that "go together," is the search for a fatality in a domain where fatality was never before a question. (How many poets writhe in their graves at the thought of how their verse has been used!)

Thus, when commissioned to write a sizeable work specifically for tenor and piano trio, I was clear about the limitations and advantages of the drama I would build, but vague about the literary impulse for the drama. I had, so to speak, the colors and the canvas, but no model.

After weeks of returning to every poet I've ever loved, foraging especially among those I'd never used (a rarefied task: To date I've set to music 120 separate poets, some of them dozens of times), finally only W. H. Auden seemed inevitable. Then, the choice of *which* Auden required days of re-reading.

Why did I settle on these seven famous poems, all from his so-called middle period? Because, as we Quakers say, they spoke to my condition. Each is an admixture of cynicism and vulnerability, of force and hopelessness, of hot sadness and cold joy, of an objectivity that nevertheless surges. Whether writing of the Trojan War—which could as well be the Vietnam War for all we've learned meanwhile—or of a modern romance between two petty lovers who are nonetheless sanctified, Auden's wry pen is master, there's something to sing about, and one thing leads to another.

Once the texts were decided upon, the musical parturition occurred during a mere seven weeks, from June 21 to August 16, 1989, in Nantucket.

1990

The Third Quartet

There is no First Quartet. Well, actually there *is*, but it's a student endeavor stashed forever in a drawer with many another of my opus-minus-ones. However, since my first real string quartet, which dates from 1950, is published under the title "Second Quartet," I have no choice but to name the present work "Third Quartet." Forty years separate these two pieces. The interim contains a hefty amount of chamber music, much of it including—but none of it exclusively for—string quartet.

The Third Quartet comprises the following sections: *Chaconne, Scherzo-Sarabande-Scherzo, Dirge-Dance-Dirge, Epitaph,* and *Dervish.*

The Chaconne's "ground," uttered in the high reaches of the Second Violin, is a sequence of twelve notes (B, F-sharp, A, F, B-flat, E, E-flat, D, A-flat, G, C, C-sharp) requiring one slow measure apiece. The resulting dozen measures are repeated seven times, unchanged, and expressionless as the sky. Against this neutral background ambiguous disturbances occur: Is the First Violin an eagle swerving? Is the Viola a block of clouds, and the Cello an oceanic eruption? These disturbances combine, agitate, and eventually fade as they had come, while the indifferent sky remains forever. The musical material is all derived from the "sky" motive, but played backward by the First Violin, and radically transposed—and sometimes upside-down—by Viola and Cello.

The plucked tune tossed about through the second movement is again derived from the original twelve tones. Counterpointing this is a scurrying figure of five descending notes which, after ninety seconds, subsides into a formal *Sarabande*—actually the *Scherzo* in slow motion. After two and a half minutes the *Sarabande* melts back into its former whispering shape.

Dirge is concocted from a roughish two-bar chorale stated thrice, each statement followed by a solo cadenza. Now comes a second theme, spacious and sustained, accompanied by a murmur growing toward a torrent that finally bursts into a rhythmic dance. The *Dance* is a speeded-up—a "released"—version of the *Dirge* to which, for reasons of proprietary symmetry, it returns, and all ends softly.

Epitaph, brief and motionless, is a song without words depicting a child's tombstone on a sunny afternoon. *Dervish* is a *perpetuum mobile* surrounding a canon based on the "sky" motive which, after persistent reiterations, whirls to a close.

(Let me stress that although I speak of a twelve-note motive, this is indeed a motive and not a row in the Schoenbergian sense. My music is profoundly tonal, and so to my ear is all music, tonality being a law of the universe.)

The foregoing information is more visually illustrative than is my wont when discussing non-vocal music, but lately I've found such descriptions useful. Hitherto my habit has been to give just the facts, such as: The Third Quartet, a thirty-minute piece in five movements, was commissioned by the June Festival of Albuquerque as a gift for the Guarneri Quartet. It was composed during the last five months of 1990, in Nantucket, Saratoga Springs, and New York City.

1991

Fourth String Quartet

Yes, Picasso's paintings did impel this suite, yet to subtitle it "Picasso" seems nervy and irrelevant (nervy, in hitching my wagon to the great man's star; irrelevant, in that no music irrefutably depicts other than itself). But yes again, composers do often seek to conjoin their art with another art—with the poetry of song, for instance, and more exceptionally with the visual, by representing through sound their special "Pictures at an Exhibition." So when the chips are down, will I remove the titles and simply offer my work like the abstraction that it is? Or will I retain the titles? You, reading this, will know the ultimate decision—that I want it both ways.

The music came rapidly, four of the movements being composed in January of 1994, the six others during a fortnight at Yaddo in July. Most of the ten "pictures" are related thematically, and all are related—I pray—theatrically. The central piece is *Self Portrait*, which bears the interpretive suggestion: "with horror and indifference." While feeding solely off the given material, this movement means unequivocally to portray the schizoid temper of any artist—or, indeed, any human—whose hot urge for self-expression is met by the cold self-protection of his alter ego. Thus is it too, though more hidden and serene, in the nine other sections.

Now, lest this program note melt into psychobabble, I'll only add that the music was commissioned by the South Mountain Association especially for performance by the Emerson String Quartet, and that it lasts about twenty-six minutes.

1995

Evidence of Things Not Seen

(*36 Songs for 4 Solo Voices and Piano*)

Look not to things that are seen, but to that which is unseen;
For things that are seen pass away, but that which is unseen is
forever.   Corinthians II, 4:18

It is at once by poetry and through poetry, by music and through
music, that the soul divines what splendors shine beneath the
tomb.   Edgar Allan Poe
                                                  The Poetic Principle

Faith is the substance of things hoped for, the evidence of things
not seen.   Hebrews, II:1

If in the world of Elvis, song is a trillion-dollar business, in the
world of serious classical music song is the least remunerative of
expressions. Song in English, particularly by Americans, is more
rarefied still, partly because historically the form's intimacy never
meshed with the massive concepts of our pioneer composers, and
partly because we have no recital tradition for singers. You can
count on one hand the number of vocalists who subsist as recitalists, and even they prosper more than the composers. Today,
re-creation takes priority over creation.

Nevertheless, I embarked on the madness of a composer's career by writing songs. The first ones, at fourteen, were settings of Cummings. By forty I had written four hundred songs, on texts of over one hundred authors, from Anonymous to Ashbery, Freud to Kafka, Wylie to Whitman. My singular reputation, such as it is, has always centered around the song, probably because there is so little competition. Whatever my music is worth, I flatter myself that my taste in texts is first-rate. For it was not the human voice that first drew me to song (I am not obsessed with the voice, much less am I an opera buff), but poetry as expressed through the voice. I am un-American by not being a specialist; as child I never anguished about which to be when I grew up, a composer or a writer. Why not be both? (No, I don't set my own words to music, but that's another story.) If eventually I composed many a non-vocal work, such work emerged from a sense of duty: One is supposed to "branch out." Though probably every non-vocal work by every composer—be it a toccata for tuba or sonata for snare drum—is a song in disguise. Music *is* song and inside all composers lurks a singer striving to get out.

For decades I've dreamed of an *Art of the Song*, a glorified chamber piece for four solo voices with piano, to be presented as an entire program. The challenge would be less musical than theatrical. A composer always has musical ideas or he wouldn't be a composer; but when he proposes to link these abstract ideas to concrete words—words by authors who never asked to be musicalized—he must find words which (at least for him) need to be sung. If these words are intended for a cycle rather than for a single song, then there must be a sense (at least for him) of inevitability in their sequence, because the same song in a different context takes on new meaning. If the chosen words are by different authors, then these authors must seem to share a certain parenting (at least for him) even though they may be separated by centuries. (I say "words" rather than "poems," since many of the texts I use are prose.)

Last year the New York Festival of Song, in tandem with the Library of Congress, agreed to sponsor this dream. I am warmly grateful to these organizations.

In plotting the format of the present work, composed mostly in 1997, I chose thirty-six texts by twenty-four authors. Wystan Auden, Paul Goodman (a childhood idol), and Walt Whitman, all of whom I had used dozens of times before, are here represented by five, four, and three poems each. William Penn, who, as we Quakers say, "speaks to my condition," is represented by two prose selections, as are Stephen Crane and the eighteenth-century hymnodist, Thomas Ken. The other eighteen authors provide one song each. The sendoff by Roethke, "From Whence Cometh Song," I used once before in another version, and would not have set it again, but no other poem seemed more apt. The verses of Wordsworth, Browning, and Elizabeth Barrett, though world famous, are new to my pen. Edna Millay, another childhood idol, remains close to my heart. Like Penn, John Woolman was a Quaker thinker whose prose dates from the early 1700s; his pacifism, like that of the more ironic Langston Hughes, contrasts with the sometimes warlike Kipling. Kipling's contemporary countrymen, Oscar Wilde and A. E. Housman, with their Victorian poignancy, contrast in turn with the American poignancy of the very late Jane Kenyon. The prose passages from the French of Colette and of Julian Green are, in my translation, the final paragraphs respectively of their semi-autobiographical works, *L'Étoile vesper* and *L'Autre sommeil*. Robert Frost, along with Dickinson and Whitman, is probably the great American poet most often used by musicians; his elegiac "Come In" fits perfectly here. So does Baudelaire's English verse, and that of Yeats which is arranged for trio. Mark Doty's weighty harangue, "Faith," from his *Atlantis*, specifically concerns the calamity of AIDS, as does the penultimate song, drawn from the late Paul Monette's *Love Alone*.

Two of the songs, Green's "He Thinks upon His Death" and Goodman's "Boy with a Baseball Glove," were composed forty-five years ago, and have waited all this time to find a home. (In 1984, I did reshape the Goodman song, minus the words, into the third movement of a Violin Concerto.) Two of the authors still thrive: Mark Doty in Provincetown, and Julian Green, age ninety-seven, in Paris. I have personally known six of them, though none, I think, have known each other; the interrelationship depends solely on my whimsical juxtaposition, as does their continuity within the cycle.

The order of the songs relies on subject matter. The opening group, *Beginnings,* is just that—songs about moving forward, and the wistful optimism of love, with a concluding hymn-text from the eighteenth century to be sung by a congregation in the morning. (Although I am an atheist, I am sincere in my dozens of settings of so-called sacred texts; I do believe in Belief, and in the great art, starting with the Psalms of David, that has sprung from religious conviction.)

The second group, *Middles,* about coming of age, horror of war, romantic disappointment, concludes with another hymn, this one for evening. The last group, *Ends,* about death, concludes with an admonishment from William Penn, echoing a definition of Faith in Corinthians II: "Look not to things that are seen, but to that which is unseen; for things that are seen pass away, but that which is unseen is forever."

Non-vocal music is never literal, can never be proven to "mean" anything. Tone poems mean only what the composer tells you, in words, they mean, and the representation is general: the sea, love, death, weather, but never knife or green or elbow or Tuesday. Song settings, meanwhile, can mean only what their texts tell you they mean; no one composer is more right than another in his interpretation of the same text. Nevertheless, certain conventions, that shift with centuries, ascribe specific meaning to ambiguous sound. Minor modes, for instance, signify sadness, while stately rhythms signify weddings. Since words speak louder than music, but since music, precisely because of its meaninglessness, can heighten or even change the sense of words, I try, in word-settings, to avoid the conventions. I don't compose "war music" for war scenes or "love music" for love scenes, preferring to contradict — but can you prove it's a contradiction? — the expected. Thus I'm sometimes criticized for missing the point of a poem. Still, it's not for a composer to review his own music, since that music speaks louder than his words.

None of the texts is especially upbeat; even Auden's nonsensical quatrains seem less funny than scary. Ten years ago I might not have chosen them. But they now seem endemic to this autumnal moment, as I look back to a youth "which foresaw in the light of a summer day the end of all life."

1997

Double Concerto for Violin
and Cello with Orchestra

In the more than twenty-five years that we've known each other, Sharon Robinson and Jaime Laredo have performed, separately and together, a great deal of my pre-existing chamber music. Gradually they came to exemplify for me the ideal string players. Thus in 1980 I wrote, specifically for Sharon, a suite for cello alone called *After Reading Shakespeare;* five years later, at Jaime's behest, came the Violin Concerto. Now the time seemed ripe to compose something for the pair of them. And so, thanks to a commission from the Indianapolis Symphony, in the state where I was born, the present work has come to be.

Music being the least representational of the arts (it does not depict other than itself), the overall title is abstract: Double Concerto. Nevertheless, just to get the juices flowing, I did impose "concrete" titles onto the eight movements, which require thirty-five minutes to unfold. These titles connote whatever the listener chooses. I'll state only that in *Adam and Eve* the two soloists are literally born on the stage: They emerge from the womb of the orchestra.

The scoring is plain: only eight winds, four brass, and strings. No glamorous harps, keyboards, or mallets, and no percussion, none. (In growing older I've come to feel that percussion is, at best, mere decoration, at worst, immoral, like too many earrings or too many exclamation points!!)

The music was composed on the islands of Manhattan and Nantucket between July 27, 1997 and April of this year. The orchestration was completed in June.

1998

Another Sleep

> Who knows if this other half of life in which we think we are awake
> is not another sleep a little different from the first, from which we
> awaken when we think we are asleep?   Pascal

When Jim Holmes died on January 9, 1999, the world instantly
took a new meaning—or rather, a new lack of meaning. Nothing
mattered now, neither life nor death. He was nearly sixteen years
younger than I; we had lived together since 1967.

But the world goes on turning, and I'm supposed to be a composer. So I've sewn together a memorial for Jim, nineteen songs
based on texts (prose and poetry) by fourteen authors. Three of
the songs were written over a half-century ago: "Mongolian Idiot"
in January 1947 when I was twenty-three; and, two years later the
lines from Julian Green's brief memoir, *L'Autre sommeil*, translated as "Another Sleep." The others date mostly from the past
few months in Nantucket and at Yaddo.

The overall theme stresses nostalgia and loss, but also frustration and anger, and finally renewal, albeit renewal through defi-
ance of death. I'd like to think that the juxtaposition of unrelated
writers contains a certain logic, a certain balance. For instance,
the fierce cries of Cavafy and Pollitt are, as I hear them, two sides

of one coin; likewise Shakespeare's famous sonnet and Green's wistful souvenirs; Ashbery and Sappho, Borges and Goodman. But composers can explain too much. Music speaks for itself.

2000

For *Our Town*

What can be said about the music that the music can't say better? Only how it came to be written.

Prior to *Our Town* I composed seven operas (or twelve, if you count all of *Fables*). These are:

A Childhood Miracle (1951), libretto by Elliott Stein after Hawthorne's *Snow Image*, for six singers and thirteen instruments, 33 minutes.

The Robbers (1956), melodrama in one scene, for three male singers and eight instruments, libretto after Chaucer's *The Pardoner's Tale*.

Miss Julie (1965), libretto by Kenward Elmslie after Strindberg, for four solo singers, chorus, and full orchestra, two acts, two hours. Later changed to one act, 90 minutes. (This was my only full-length opera—though what does "full-length" mean? Cannot a ten-minute work be full-length?)

Bertha (1968), on Kenneth Koch's play, for mezzo-soprano, chorus, a "cast of thousands," with piano accompaniment, 25 minutes.

Three Sisters Who Are Not Sisters (1968), on a play in three scenes by Gertrude Stein, five solo singers, piano accompaniment, 35 minutes.

Fables (1970), five very short operas on poems of Jean de la Fontaine, translated by Marianne Moore. *The Lion in Love, Bird Wounded by an Arrow, Fox and the Grapes, Sun and the Frogs,* and *The Animals Sick of the Plague*, 22–28 minutes.

Hearing (1976), a libretto dramatization by James Holmes of Kenneth Koch's poems, drawn from the 1966 song cycle.

Beyond this are unpublished juvenilia: *Cain and Abel* with Paul Goodman, 1946; *Last Day,* a nine-minute monodrama with Jay Harrison, 1959; an incomplete two-acter called *The Anniversary* with Jascha Kessler, 1961; and *Four Dialogues* with Frank O'Hara, 1954. ("Juvenilia" does not mean amateurish as much as just early.)

The Dialogues, like all the other works, are published by Boosey and Hawkes, except for *A Childhood Miracle,* which is with Peer-Southern.

———

Such as it is, my reputation seems to center around vocal music (although the 1976 Pulitzer Prize was for a straight orchestral piece, *Air Music*). Besides the operas, there are perhaps 500 songs including several cycles, some with small ensembles.

It does not follow that "vocal" composers are equally comfortable in both song and opera. Puccini, Verdi, and even Wagner are not known for their songs; Fauré, Duparc, and even Brahms are not known for their operas. Some are at home in each medium: Richard Strauss, Poulenc, and even Virgil Thomson.

Myself, I'm more at ease with song. Opera is prose and spins a yarn, while song is poetry and depicts a state of mind. With a song on a pre-existing text I know the end before I begin. Whatever my songs may be worth, I flatter myself that my choice of texts is first-rate.

Do I set my own words to music—for I am an author too? No. If Ned-the-writer were good enough to please Ned-the-composer, the text would be self-sufficient, and hence untouchable.

————

Our Town by Thornton Wilder is internationally the best-known play of the twentieth century. The 1940 movie version had a heart-breakingly simple background score by Aaron Copland. Since then, many a musician, including Copland, has applied in vain for operatic rights. Did Wilder feel that the play contained its own "music," and that real music would be gilding a very fragile lily?

The idea of my doing it was not my own, but that of J. D. (Sandy) McClatchy. Sandy, friend of Wilder's nephew Tappan, executor of Thornton's estate, procured the rights and wrote the libretto. The libretto, pared down from three to two acts, and with a few set pieces, is otherwise faithful to the original.

Does it need to be sung? Am I the one to make it singable? And is it Ned-the-songwriter or Ned-the-operawriter who makes it work? As of this day, January 8, 2006, I have not heard it. Nor have you. In a month we will see—or hear—and then decide.

2006

Index